"I didn could

Lori stammered, and Brant's mouth twisted faintly.

"I told you you didn't know the first thing about being made love to! You've got to grow up sometime."

Lori sat bemused, the feelings stirring in her heart so new she wasn't even sure she wanted to own up to them. She was a sham, a total sham, and now she knew it she might be able to protect herself. Brant could, if he wished, turn her life inside out just by making love to her.

Finally she had to look at him, a flush under her golden skin. "You had no business kissing me. You only did it to shock me!"

Other titles by
MARGARET WAY
IN HARLEQUIN ROMANCES

Other titles by
MARGARET WAY
IN HARLEQUIN PRESENTS

The Awakening Flame

by

MARGARET WAY

Harlequin Books

TORONTO · LONDON · NEW YORK · AMSTERDAM
SYDNEY · HAMBURG · PARIS

Original hardcover edition published in 1978
by Mills & Boon Limited

ISBN 0-373-02203-4

Harlequin edition published October 1978

CHAPTER ONE

By the time Lori got off the bus, she was nearly faint-
ing with the heat. The trip had been rough and the
smell of dust and burning gum trees was thick in her
nostrils. A state of emergency had been declared in the
valley more than a week ago and it was still in force.
No one would be criminal enough to light an open
fire, but who could prevent the paper-dry gums from
igniting? There had been small bush fires raging all
along the highway and the swimming blue sky was
overlaid by an ominous smoke haze.

Lori's fear of fire was shared by all the hardworking
community. For the last two days there had been a
heavy billowing haze on the eastern slopes of Barradon
and the local radio station had been kept busy broadcasting warnings, calls and directions to homesteaders
and volunteer firefighters. The worst outbreaks were
some distance away so there was no immediate danger,
but Lori would be glad to get back to the farm and
know it was safe.

It was a new idea and a very unpleasant one, but she
was convinced Dianne wouldn't care. Four years away
had changed Dianne beyond all recognition. There
was no softness in her now, but an acerbic wit and a
ruthless determination to gratify her own desires. She
had no sense of community or love of the land, and
Lori was almost certain she found the rural life intolerable. The hectic, much-travelled years spent as a
highly successful fashion model had given Dianne the
gloss of a pearl, but it was clear she thought only an

idiot like Lori would live on a farm. Still, it was the
first time she had ever bothered to come back to see
her father and the young cousin her parents had
reared from the age of twelve, and thinking this, Lori
stifled her momentary flash of anger. Uncle Viv had
to be protected at all costs, and if he thought his
daughter perfect, Lori wasn't going to disillusion him.

Wearily she took off her sunglasses and rubbed a
trickle of sweat from her small, straight nose. No sign
of Uncle Viv or the pick-up when the sight of either
would have been very welcome. The bus had been late
too, and already the small crowd of passengers was
dispersing. Probably with Dianne home, Uncle Viv
had forgotten all about her, despite the fact that Lori
had travelled into the Junction to complete some of
the farm's pressing business. Uncle Viv's little lapses
of memory were troubling her of late and she knew
quite well that Dianne would never offer her services
to drive into the town to pick up her cousin. Just
thinking about Dianne and the jarring way she had
behaved since she had arrived back at the farm made
Lori click her tongue. Though she might wish and
wish things could be different between them, she
knew quite well wishes were as useless as dreams.
Dianne always had resented her, and she didn't know
why.

Parrots and parakeets screamed overhead and Lori
lifted her eyes to the trees. Jacarandas formed a
shimmering violet-blue avenue right down the main
street and shading the front of the shire council
chambers opposite were a trio of magnificent poincianas, their branches laden with great crimson trusses
of flowers. How they defied the extraordinary dry
heat! Lori almost forgot her discomfort for the delight
of the trees. They lent an exquisite illusion of coolness

even when the sun's brilliance was making her slit her eyes defensively. When she got home she would have to change into something really bare, a halter-neck and shorts. Bellara just missed the sugar belt to the north, but it shared a good deal of its sweltering weather.

If the worst came to the worst, and it looked very much like it, she would have to ring Dean and ask him to run her back to the farm. Though Dean's mother wouldn't permit much of a relationship to blossom, Lori knew Dean was falling in love with her. It seemed a pity to use him when she felt only sympathy and liking, but it was much too far to walk, and absolutely killing in the savage heat. She would wait another half hour in the air-conditioned depot, then she would consider again.

Head down, disconsolate, she was cutting her way between two erratically parked vehicles when an imperative, male voice hailed her:

'Lori!'

She froze in her tracks and even considered not answering at all. But what good would that do? Brant Elliot invariably got his way and he had constituted himself some kind of a watchdog, especially since Dianne had come home. She turned a little awkwardly, if a small, graceful girl could do that, and saw him open out the door of his big, expensive station wagon parked much further along. A minute later he swung out and was walking towards her, while she tried to ignore his height and his width of shoulder. Brant Elliot was a head taller than most men and the sight of him and the crisp, authoritative sound of his voice literally put her teeth on edge.

'What's the rush?'

She tilted her head to look up at him. All six feet three of him exuded a hard male arrogance that made her feel endangered. He was the most disturbing human being she had ever met, but he had a totally different effect on Dianne. She found him dynamic.

'Well?' One black eyebrow shot up interrogatively.

'I was just going into the depot to wait for Uncle Viv.'

'He won't be coming, little one!'

'Now how would you know that?' His slightly mocking smile was making her blood boil, as usual.

'I've just come from the farm. Dianne is over at Camfield and Viv was just setting out to pick her up. It appears, my lamb, he forgot all about you.'

'Never mind!' Lori said shortly. 'I'll ring Dean.'

'Oh no, you won't!' One lean hand shot out decisively and forcibly detained her. 'Not when I've come in especially!'

'For goodness' sake!' she marvelled sarcastically. 'So I've got more than I bargained for?'

'It seems like it, carrot-top!'

She put her free hand to her flowing Titian hair. 'Which instantly sums me up, I suppose?'

'You *do* have a quick boiling point,' he remarked drily. 'But don't let's stand around in the sun sparring—it's too hot. Any luggage?'

'No.' As usual he made her feel distraught, disordered, defensive and flaming with life.

'Then come along with me. It's the best way.'

'And it's so good of you to offer!'

His blue-green eyes had the glitter of aquamarines. 'One of these days, Lori, I'm going to drop you in a deep waterhole.'

'That's all right, I'm a good swimmer.'

'And you're very inexperienced with men.'

She shrugged her delicate shoulders and said pointedly, 'I'll survive.'

'Are you so sure of that?'

He was towering above her, but she couldn't retreat; he had too firm a grip on her arm. 'You just like needling me, Brant. I wish you wouldn't.'

'It must make a nice change from young Stanton?'

Relentlessly he was bearing her along with him and she said rather heatedly, 'Leave Dean alone. Anyway, he's brilliant!'

'So I've heard!' Brant glanced down at her glistening head, seeing the effect of the sun on the bright silky tendrils. 'Didn't he have a breakdown or something and needs looking after?'

Lori's amber eyes sparked up at him. 'It's a pity you don't show a bit more sympathy for those less endowed than yourself. Dean isn't strong. The concert life doesn't suit everyone. He's an amazingly gifted pianist, he always was, but he's exceedingly sensitive!'

'And that's your line, is it? Being sympathetic?'

'Not really!' she said shortly. 'You can't imagine how I feel about you.'

'And it just might have some embarrassing consequences for yourself—so don't tip that determined little chin at me, and don't tangle with Stanton. He'll drain all your strength, and I don't think his mother will ever be persuaded to let him go.'

'Anything else you'd like to talk about?'

With gentle violence he put her into the big estate car. 'Was it exciting at Junction?'

'As dead as a cemetery!'

Brent laughed under his breath, then walked to the other side of the car, slipping into the driver's seat beside her. The engine sprang to life and he reversed expertly out of a tricky position. 'It's not not quite fair Viv going off for Dianne when you do all the work,' he murmured quite affably.

'She's his daughter, after all.'

'And you're his little business manager and you damn near run the farm.'

Lori put up her slender young arms as if in an incantation. 'Please, Brant, it's too hot. Besides I'm exhausted.'

'You don't look it!' His brilliant, mocking gaze flicked her face and her throat. 'You're a delectable little creature really. Pity you don't make the most of yourself.'

'Like Dianne?' she asked sweetly.

'She hasn't got *your* hair!'

'For which she's grateful!'

He made a jeering little noise in his throat. 'My darling child, let me wipe out the terrible taunts of you childhood. Your hair isn't *horrible*, it's fabulous, though I can see you don't entirely believe me. What does Stanton have to say?'

'Whatever it is, I'm going to keep it to myself!'

'And have a care!' he returned rather curtly. 'Stanton's been protected by a possessive woman all his life. Actually his problem is extremely interesting, but too big for one little chick!'

Lori sighed voluptuously and let her head fall back against the seat. 'You're a damnable man! There's no respite, is there?'

'Someone has to warn you!' he returned mildly.

'I know how to take care of myself!'

'Really? You're not a very big girl.'

'That isn't what I meant. You mustn't confuse inches with common sense.'

'I'm sorry, I forgot!' His brilliant glance burned in the air and Lori turned her head abruptly to look out at the old familiar landmarks, the pub and the bank, the civic centre and the library. The town never changed. It always looked the same, eternally countrified, pleasant and prosperous. Junction was much bigger, the commercial centre for the coast and the hinterland.

'I don't like this drought!' she said as they made a left turn for the highway.

'Who does? If we don't get some rain soon we're all in real trouble—I've never seen anything more frightening than those whipping gum trees alight. Every twig and branch that flies off ignites where it lands.'

'At least the highway is a natural fire break!'

'Don't count on it!' he said grimly. 'I told Viv I was sending a few men across to clear some of your land. He hardly heard me.'

'I'll bet he was grateful!'

His vibrant voice sounded quite hard. 'I don't want gratitude, Lori. I want a more responsible attitude. Dianne doesn't seem to have any idea of the dangers. She's not in the least like you.'

'We were raised differently!' Lori explained. 'Dianne went away to boarding school and I stayed at home with Aunt Jocelyn and Uncle Viv. He hasn't been the same since Aunt Jocelyn died, and to make it worse Dianne left home shortly after that.'

'Now you're all he's got. He should take more care of you.'

'He *does*!' Lori protested as though this was blasphemy. 'You can't know how good Uncle Viv was, how kind and understanding!'

'All right, all right!' He reached out a hand and patted her shoulder. 'Simmer down, little one. Your uncle isn't the man he was, you must realise that?'

As much as she agreed, Lori preferred to rebuke him. 'I know you'd like the farm!' she said heatedly.

'*Shut up!*'

'Why? Are you afraid to bring it out in the open?'

'I thought I had from time to time with you hovering anxiously right outside the door. The fact is, Lori, you've got a good property that's going to ruin despite your valiant efforts. Your uncle has lost all interest and he's been running at a loss for a time now. Another bad season will break him. You know my terms and I think they're quite reasonable. I don't want to put Viv out of his home. He's welcome to the house for the rest of his life. I simply want the land. To *work* it, not waste it. I'll put it to cotton.'

'Oh yes, you're not without wealth and power, but what the hell do you expect *me* to do?' she demanded.

'My dear,' he said kindly, 'you'll marry.'

Lori laughed appreciatively, a bitter-sweet little sound. 'Thanks very much!'

'*I'm* not proposing.'

'That's fine. You're thirty-four to my twenty.'

'Yes, but women get the worst of it, don't they?'

'I'll admit it,' she shrugged.

'That's very generous of you, Lori, but at the moment you're a beautiful young girl.'

'Oh, don't be ridiculous!' she said wearily. 'I'm *not*!'

'Then you're not as smart as I like to give you credit for,' drawled Brant.

'It would be easy to hate you!' she breathed. 'I think you'd better accept that you can't have the farm and even *you* can be made to learn to take no for an answer!'

'Little fool!' His self-confidence was unshakeable. 'You're gallant, I'll grant you that, but one small girl can't run a property. You're going to lose your youth and your health, and I don't like it. Look at your hands!'

'I don't want to. I know they're rough, but I try to look after them.'

'How can you, *labouring*?' He muffled a strong exclamation. 'As far as I can make out Dianne gets what little extra money there is when it seems to me she should be sending something home for her father. He's not a young man and he adores her. You might finish with nothing.'

'And I don't care!' Lori said doggedly. 'Aunt Jocelyn and Uncle Viv raised me. What I'm doing now is a small return for the long years of unselfish loving care!'

'Oh, bravo!' he taunted her. 'Little Saint Lorinda!'

'Certainly not!' Lori made a sharp impatient sound. 'I'm just deeply involved.'

'And won't listen to sense. Despite your spirited little way you're really a martyr. That's why I'm coming over so frequently.'

'Naturally!' she said drily. 'It's not to see Dianne.'

'Is that *really* what you think?' he asked smoothly, and she felt a shoot of anger rip through her. The sun had darkened his skin to mahogany, gilding the hard, classical features, the deeply cleft chin. She didn't understand her fear of him, but she realised Dianne would fit in very well with his way of life. Dianne *was* beautiful and she had become very sophisticated and aware of her own power. Also she had decided Brant Elliot was the first man in her life she really wanted. Probably if he had been in the Valley four years ago she would never have left.

Lori stared sombrely out of the window at the flying miles. All around them, the undulating hills and grasslands were scorched to a rich crackling gilt. They had missed out on the spring rains and the summer had been long and dry. Drought was an insatiable thing, merciless like the glare of the sun. The trees were withering and losing their leaves and soon there would be no shade at all for the suffering cattle. No one felt at all optimistic about rain, and Lori's smooth forehead pleated anxiously. The least little unattended spark could set the country ablaze.

Brant was a rich man. He could withstand heavy losses, for his investments covered a wide area; beef and timber, field crops like sunflower and cotton, and he even had an interest in a pineapple plantation that yielded record crops. Brant didn't have to worry unduly, but the farm was all but finished; Lori's trip to Junction had confirmed that. Mr Sommerville had looked over the top of his glasses at her and sympathetically drawn little red crosses all over his blotter. Uncle Viv was no business man and over the last few years he had lost much of his health and vigour. It was only since Aunt Jocelyn died that Lori came to realise it was her aunt who had really run the farm and made it pay. Aunt Jocelyn had quietly decided everything, and now Uncle Viv was going downhill bit by bit, dying slowly of a broken heart. Though he blinded himself to the fact, Dianne was scarcely a loving or considerate daughter and though he loved Lori and often commended her for her hard work, the centre of his world had fallen out with his wife's death. He no longer bothered to ride out into the shadeless bush, and once or twice lately he had even called Lori *Jocelyn* by mistake.

Lori too had an achingly clear picture of her aunt. It was Aunt Jocelyn who had taught her to be self-sufficient, to know and trust herself. Aunt Jocelyn had been her own mother's eldest sister and she had reared Lori not as a duty but with much love and understanding. Aunt Jocelyn had been the strong one, a good woman, and Lori sorely missed her.

'Why the heartfelt sigh?' asked Brant.

'Oh, I was just thinking about days gone past.'

'Your aunt?'

'How did you know?' Startled, she turned to stare at him, her great amber eyes shadowed pools of light.

'The expression on your face jolted some of my own memories. She must have been a wonderful woman?'

'She was!' Lori said in a softly tender tone. 'She was even tolerant of all my odd little bursts of temperament. My parents were killed in a car smash a few miles from our home. There were others in the family circle, but Aunt Jocelyn offered immediately to have me. She more than anyone made me whole again after the tragedy.'

'Poor little orphan!'

'I still am.'

He glanced at her profile, assessing her mood. 'You're lonely.'

'I'm *not*, but I'm flattered you actually bothered to come in for me. I didn't know you had that much feeling.'

'On the contrary, little one, I have very strong feelings. I just can't afford to indulge them.' He turned his head briefly, his dark face saturnine. There was an expression in the blue-green eyes that was very hard to interpret.

'Now that's really interesting!' Lori said flippantly. 'You might tell!'

'Forget it! You've got too much growing up to do.'

His tone was so frankly cutting she felt her eyelids sting with tears. Her own reaction horrified her and she said shakily, 'That was rather cruel!'

'But I *am* cruel, young Lori. Didn't you know?' He

saw the shimmer of tears in her beautiful eyes and his mouth twisted with amused exasperation. 'Poor little scrap, I've hurt you.'

'And it's just the sort of thing you like to do. Why do you expect so much from me?'

'I'm damned if I know. Don't worry, I find it as irritating as you do!'

Lori looked very carefully out of the window. A woman could get burned tangling with Brant Elliot, yet most of the women in the district cried after him, Dianne included. As a bachelor he could graciously bestow his favours where he pleased. Other women might vibrate like aspens over him, but Lori found him disagreeable, and there was no use pretending otherwise.

Before long they turned off the highway on to the private road Brant had built and graciously allowed them to use. The long drive took them past the low, rambling, beautiful old homestead built long ago by Brant's great-uncle from whom he had inherited the property and a good deal of valuable land scattered over the vast hinterland. Unlike the farm where only the native bougainvilleas sprawled in brilliant cascades, the large garden in front of the house was beautiful, with shade trees and all kinds of flowering shrubs, and even the sweeping expanse of lawn was in far better condition than anyone else's.

Lori remained silent, conscious of a strange hurting feeling within her. They wound in and out, flashing between the avenues of trees, and there wasn't a single inch of the boundary fence that wasn't in splendid condition. Brant was blessed with enormous drive and a capacity for hard work that impressed everyone, and the prosperity of the district depended largely upon him one way or the other. It was a miracle to have inherited all this, but as far as Brant was concerned it was only the beginning. In a series of coups that triumphed over enormous difficulties he had reclaimed and irrigated vast areas of land and made it productive for field crops, and his admirers in the State were legion. No wonder he was shocked by the state of the farm and wanted to rehabilitate it. Brant was the aristocrat of the district, and Lori wondered why he bothered helping people he in some way despised.

In the distance, the main gate leading to the farm stood off its hinges and a long rail of the fence plunged to the ground and was covered with creepers. It was then that Brant laughed shortly:

'Can't that useless Albie fix that?'

'He's overworked as it is,' Lori told him.

His mouth curved into the smile she disliked. 'I'm going to offer to get someone to fix that and you're going to let me.'

'We can pay!'

'I might expect it!' Unexpectedly he pulled off the roadway and they were enveloped in an archway of deepest shade. It was oddly still and quiet, and Lori turned to him anxiously.

'What's the matter?' she asked.

Brant stared at her for a moment and his eyes were brilliant with colour. 'You sound as if you're frightened?'

She seemed to be reeling under the heavy impact of his personality. 'Let's say vaguely uneasy. I'm not going to let you talk me into anything about the farm.'

'The *farm*, my God!' A kind of hard recklessness lay on him. 'I'll have the farm before I'm finished. What I want to speak to you about is this. You've lived on my boundary for all of your life and you've only been up to the house once or twice.'

'I don't expect you to ask me.'

'Oh, don't be so damned humble!' He put out a hand and tweaked her hair hard. 'Dianne's only been back a few weeks and I see her every other day.'

Because she makes it her business, Lori thought, but naturally didn't say it. 'I have work to do!' she managed drily.

'But you've no excuse for the night-time?'

'That's what you think!'

His light eyes blazed suddenly and he put his hand on her arm. 'I wouldn't expect you to act like a woman, only an obstinate child!'

She shrugged. 'Why take any notice of me?'

His smile hardened into dark insolence. 'The whole situation gets me. You're growing up like little Ragged Ann!'

'You're a brutal devil, aren't you?' There were shadows under the tilted cheekbones and hurt in her wide amber eyes. 'Thanks for the lift.'

'I haven't finished!' he said harshly, and his voice flicked at her like a whip. 'The truth is often cruel, Lori, but strangely enough I want to help you. I'm having two women relations staying with me for an indefinite period and I'm giving a party for them this week-end—Saturday night, to be exact. You're invited, and the rest of your family. Maybe we can get Stanton along to entertain us. I'm sure he'd stir himself if he knew you were going to be there.'

'I can't answer at the moment!'

'Oh yes, you will!' he said grimly, 'otherwise you know precious little about good manners.'

She went to turn her head away and he caught the point of her chin. 'Is it so difficult?'

'You said it yourself. Ragged Ann! I'm in your debt for telling me.' It was intolerable to have him touching her and she jerked away with nervous intensity.

'You mean you haven't got a dress?'

'Oh, shut up!' she said a little wildly. 'Dianne will be thrilled to go, isn't that enough?'

The turbulence seemed to die out of his jewel-coloured eyes. 'The answer's simple enough. I'll get you one.'

Lori gave a muffled little exclamation and tried to open the door, but he reached over and gripped her shoulders. 'Good God, Lori, can't we find a way around this?'

'*Let me go!*' she exclaimed, her slender body brittle and breakable, poised away from him.

'I will when you answer.'

His voice was quiet but implacable and she half turned towards him, her heart unaccountably turning over and over. Some queer ache inside her allowed him to shape the contour of her shoulder. Again she was conscious of his arrogant, impenetrable maleness, yet despite it she was afraid of his attraction, had always been afraid of it.

'Lori?'

She saw the tautness come into his face, the glance he flashed over her eyes and her mouth and the innocent seductive cleft of her breast, then with all her strength she twisted away from him. He was too vital and alive, almost barbaric, and he made her feel the same wildness. She was out of the car and running, but she couldn't seem to move her legs, they were shaking so much. She swayed and Brant's tall figure was beside her, his expression grim.

'That was a mistake!' he said rebukingly. 'You can't run away from me, and not in this heat!'

'Yes, that was stupid.' Her apricot-tinted skin had

paled alarmingly, but nothing could quench the matchless fire of her hair.

'Come back to the car. I'll take you straight up to the house.'

She drew a single shuddering breath and went back with him. His hard, beautiful mouth had thinned to a straight line, the blue-green eyes without a flicker of warmth in them. 'I'm sorry!' she found herself saying. 'I never do seem to be able to please you.'

'No, you're not very good at it!' he agreed with the old devastating cruelty.

She waited until he was back beside her in the car, then she said quietly, 'If the invitation is still open I'd be happy to come.'

'Little martyr!'

She swallowed and held her fist in a tight little grip. 'I said I'm sorry!'

'And I guess I have to accept it. Let's make a deal. Those macramé wall hangings and plant holders or whatever—I'll buy a couple of them off you. That one in the hallway I like.'

Lori jerked her head sideways as though he had said something unheard-of, but his expression was quite serious. 'But that's the best thing I've done. It took an awful lot of time.'

'I'm sure it did, but you see, that's the one I want.'

'I don't know!' Lori said abstractedly. 'I mean, if you're trying to make it easy for me to make a little money...'

'My dear, I'm not that generous. The damned thing just pleases me.'

'It's odd for you to mention it,' she commented.

'Yes or no?'

'Yes!' she said, dictated by common sense. 'With

only a little profit for me it will cost you round about sixty dollars!'

'I expected that.'

'Did you?'She looked as ingenuous as a child.

'Mmm. I might as well collect it now. What would you like, cash or a cheque?'

'It really would have to be cash. Thank you very much.'

'I've got a few places too for those plant-holders. In fact I've really set my heart on them!'

From anger he plainly seemed to be enjoying himself, and Lori was quite startled by the change in his manner. He sounded almost indulgent, and she was faintly embarrassed by his interest in her accomplishment. At least she had the satisfaction of knowing her wall hangings in particular were very much admired, and it was something to do to fill in the evenings.

'I'm not surprised!' she said breezily. 'People often stop me in the street and ask for them. I can let you have two, actually, for nothing. You say some unspeakable things, but you do have the odd kind moment.'

'It's a miracle you realise it!' he answered drily. 'Without *your* odd moment of acting like a woman I don't know what I'd do!' He smiled at her and the effect was so devastating she even smiled back at him. 'We'd better go now while we're still in accord.'

A few minutes later they were pulling up in front of the house, a far cry from Brant's magnificent Colonial-style dwelling. The front door stood open and Lori looked at him quickly.

'They must be home. You're coming in, of course?'

He turned on her abruptly and his glance raked her

small, anxious face. 'Why are you so damned nervous?'

'Dear me, dear me!' she sighed. 'I knew it couldn't last!'

'It would with anyone else but you. Anyway, I've got a case of fruit for you in the back and I want to pick up that wall hanging. I have just the spot for it. You'll get your money tomorrow. All right?'

'Sure!' Her tender young mouth thinned a little. 'Sixty dollars should be enough to make me presentable!'

'With it or without it you'd be that! I'm only pointing out that you're entitled to one or two luxuries so don't go spending it on the house. I admire all the little changes you make, but this time spend the money on yourself!'

'My prince!' she said simply.

'I'll bring that up again, but five years from now!'

He got out of the station wagon looking tolerantly exasperated, while Dianne, like a vision, came gliding through the open doorway and down the short flight of steps.

'Brant!' she cried huskily. 'The one man in the world I want to see!'

'How exciting!' He turned and took her outstretched hand. 'How come you look more delicious every day?'

I could tell you! Lori half muttered beneath her breath and went to get out of the car, but Brant just as gallantly turned back and opened the door for her.

'There you are, little one! Safely delivered from the town.'

'Darling!' Dianne said charmingly. 'We're so sorry. Dad and I just forgot. I was over at Camfield seeing Gavin.'

'That's all right!' Lori succeeded in looking unruffled. 'I'd be the last person to want to keep you cooped up at the farm.'

'Bless your little heart!' Dianne was still hanging gracefully on Brant's arm. She looked away from her cousin and spoke to him. 'Thank you so much for picking Lori up, but we were sure she'd ring Dean. They have a thing going, by the way.'

'Why didn't someone tell *me*!' Lori retorted sharply, and moved ahead of them on to the veranda. Dianne's silvery tinkle of laughter followed her and knowing she would add a little something to that surprising bit of information Lori charged into the house. At least it was cool and tidy and there was a drink in the house to offer a guest. Uncle Viv emerged from the office, his worn face brightening the moment he saw her.

'Petty, I'm sorry. You went right out of my head!'

Lori went towards him and accepted his welcoming kiss. 'I don't know what I'm going to do with you!'

'You're a good girl, Lori!' he said quietly. 'How did it go with Sommerville?'

'I'll have to tell you later. Brant's here!'

'Oh, really? He stayed on, did he?'

'Why not?' Lori returned drily. 'Dianne's taking care of him. I'll just freshen up and come back again. It was frightfully hot on the bus.'

'They seem to be enjoying themselves!' Uncle Viv murmured, looking around brightly. 'It's wonderful to have Dianne here.'

'Yes, it is. Why don't you go through to them, darling?'

'All right, I will. I've been meaning to ask Brant's advice, so I might as well do it now. Fetch a drink for him, Lori, there's a good girl.'

'Yes, I will. Would you like anything yourself?'

'Just a beer to be sociable. Di doesn't drink!'

'I didn't know that!' Lori returned lightly, thinking of the disappearing Scotch.

In her room, she remained for a moment, staring at herself in the mirror. Brant had said beautiful. She leaned closer. No, not beautiful. Her mouth was too full, her chin too determined, her teeth were excellent, her eyes large and bright, but there were a few freckles across the bridge of her nose. She couldn't bear to look at her hair, but at least her lashes and brows were naturally dark. Dianne was the beautiful one, a tall, cool blonde with the unexpectedness of brown eyes.

Lori came away from the mirror in disgust. She didn't have time for such things. She picked up a brush, tidied her bright hair, twitched her short, ruffled skirt straight and crossed to the bathroom to splash cold water over her face and wrists. That was better! Dianne always looked like a lily in the heat while she always looked as though she was about to catch fire.

In the kitchen she hastily pulled down a tray, assembled a few glasses, their best in Brant's honour, took beer and soft drinks from the refrigerator and emptied some golden Queensland nuts into a pottery bowl. She was just getting it all together when Dianne swept into the room, pulling the door gently shut after her.

'You've taken your time!' she drawled.

'Look here, you could have done it!' snapped Lori.

'I don't bother with things like that!'

'Lord no. Would you like to take the tray in and pretend you do?'

Dianne, much the taller girl, took a few steps

nearer. 'Why do you run after Brant?' she asked. 'It's sickening and very embarrassing!'

'On the contrary, this was a special occasion. I was stranded in the town.'

Dianne made an effort to control herself, but the anger was still in her face. It didn't suit her as Lori's flaming bursts suited a redhead and her dark eyes were brilliant and a little wild. 'You know perfectly well I come first around here. You may have been Mother's favourite, but you're certainly not Dad's. Anyway, you could have rung Dean.'

Lori almost slumped against the table. 'Peace, cousin, I'm not after your dreadful Brant!'

Dianne's chiselled mouth formed a laugh. 'I should think not! You'd be completely out of the running.'

'While you've got everything arranged?'

Dianne's tiered cotton skirt swirled around her lovely long legs. 'What are you complaining about? You've got a home. You've had one for years. And you've got Dean Stanton if you want him. Just keep out of my affairs, if you've got any sense.'

'I'll remember!' said Lori drily.

Dianne continued to watch her for a moment and Lori couldn't believe she was jealous. Ever since her earliest childhood Lori had considered her cousin the most beautiful creature she had ever seen, but she wasn't all wide-eyed about her nature. Dianne could be ugly when her strange moods were upon her.

'I think we'd better go outside, don't you?' she said.

Dianne brooded for a moment, then irritably took the tray. 'Hold the door open for me. And one other thing—find some excuse for staying home Saturday night. Your cheap little dresses will look ghastly up at the house, and I imagine Brant's relatives are very superior types!'

'It never occurred to me they wouldn't be!' Lori said gamely, resisting Dianne's spite. She moved quickly and went out through the kitchen door, holding it open. 'After you, cousin!'

A warm scented breeze stirred through the hallway, lifting a lock of Dianne's hair away from her beautifully made-up face. Lori was always amazed that such an elaborate make-up should stay so perfect in the heat. Her own inexpensive brand didn't have that agreeable effect. In fact, after several frustrated efforts she didn't wear it. Maybe with a little extra money in her purse she could afford to indulge herself.

Brant took the tray from Dianne and thanked her, while she gave a gentle shrug to imply that it was all in the day's work. Uncle Viv in his quiet dignified way was smiling gently and it was obvious he admired their visitor immensely, even when he made a fuss about what needed doing and Lori's lack of social life. It was this thought that made Uncle Viv look up at Lori and smile.

'Brant's just invited us to a party. You two girls can go and represent the family. I'm too old now for that kind of thing. There'll be swimming and dancing and whatnot. It will be good for you, Lori, to get out.'

'I'm afraid she's already got a date!' Dianne said apologetically. 'Dean's been pestering the life out of her to take a run in to that awful cabaret at the Junction. You said you'd go, didn't you, pet?'

'Not a bit!' Brant broke in suavely. 'Much too much drinking goes on there. Anyway, I'm asking Stanton myself. I've been told he's a wonderful pianist and I'm sure we'll all thoroughly enjoy him if he can be persuaded to play.'

'Well then, it's all settled!' Dianne said after a moment, and turned away slightly to hide her expression. 'Do we have to get all dolled up, Brant?'

He drained the icy cold beer and set the glass down. 'That was wonderful! No, something easy, Dianne, and bring your swimsuit. We can't have a barbecue, of course, but smörgasbord is still in fashion. You'll like Jane and her mother. Both of them are charming women and they know exactly how to put guests at ease. Jane lost her husband in a yachting accident about two years ago. You probably read about it in the papers—he was Hugh Gifford, the M.P.'

'Yes, I remember now,' Uncle Viv said slowly. 'They ran into a cyclone and went aground on the Reef.'

Brant nodded. 'There were no survivors. The miracle was Jane wasn't with him. Anyway, the tragedy was almost her undoing. She was pregnant and she lost the baby. It was only her wonderful courage that kept her going, and she's very close to Ruth, her mother. I've invited them to stay as long as they like, but now I'm not so sure I should have with the heat and the fire risk.'

'I'm sure they'll love it!' Dianne said enthusiastically. 'The house is air-conditioned and with any luck at all we'll get a few storms to cool us down.'

'Right!' said Brant, and stood up. 'I'd better get going. If it's all right with you, Viv, I'll get the men to move in some time tomorrow.'

'It's really very good of you!' Uncle Viv struggled to his feet and Lori noticed not for the first time that his circulation seemed to be poor.

'No problem. They know the general layout of the property. We'll just fell some of that scrub.'

'Don't touch the paperbarks!' Lori said swiftly, and Uncle Viv grunted in amusement.

'Lori loves her trees!'

'You need a few good shade trees around the house,' Brant said easily. 'I could let you have a few advanced saplings.'

Lori was just wondering when she or Albie would find the time to put them in when Brant turned his dark head and pinned her gaze. 'The men might as well put them in at the same time. Otherwise Lori here will knock herself out digging holes!'

'Don't worry, she enjoys it!' Dianne gave her tinkling peal of laughter and looked at Lori fondly. 'Short on glamour, our Lori, but a proper little scrubber!'

Uncle Viv evidently didn't quite like this, for he said very firmly, 'She's my right hand and she knows it!'

Dianne started to explain that she was only teasing when Brant remembered the wall hanging Lori had been hoping and hoping he would forget. 'By the way, Lori, what about that wall hanging you promised me? It should look very effective against the back terrace wall.'

Dianne arched her eyebrows in amazement. 'You're not serious, Brant? Lori only does these things for fun!'

'As a matter of fact she's sold quite a few!' Uncle Viv butted in. 'Very clever with her hands, is Lori, just like my dear wife. Why, just look how she's brightened up around here. It suits a woman to be artistic.'

'Surely it's easy enough if one follows instructions!' Dianne got up in one smooth movement, and the shoulder of her expensive drawstring blouse fell provocatively off one alabaster slope. Dianne never tanned and thought the kiss of the sun disastrous. 'Do tell us, which one do you mean?'

'Naturally the best!' Lori said drily. 'The one in the hallway. My very best effort!'

'I usually go for the best as a rule!' The blue-green eyes touched Lori's face lightly and Dianne came swiftly to stand at his side.

'How *nice* you are, Brant! Lori does need a little encouragement at that!'

'You'll have to get it down.' Lori couldn't bear to look at them and walked out into the hallway. They looked a stunningly attractive couple, one so dark and the other so exquisitely fair.

'You're not taking any money for this, are you, pet?' Uncle Viv came up unobtrusively behind her.

'I was going to.'

'But Brant's so good to us!'

'I know, dear. But he insists on paying!'

'Ah well,' Uncle Viv began to chew on his lip, 'I suppose you'll need a little extra for the party. God knows where the money goes around here!'

'I'll tell you if you've got time!' Lori tried to shake the macramé panel loose from the hook, but Brant came behind her.

'Can't you learn to accept a little help?'

'Gosh, I've given myself a crick in the neck!'

'Well, don't blame me!' Effortlessly he unhooked the panel and folded it over his arm, all the wooden beads making a dull clacking noise. 'You don't know what this means to me, Lori.'

'Beast!'

Dianne's dark watchful eyes swept over their faces, but whatever she saw it made her relax. 'I'll come down to the car with you, Brant. I suppose I'll see you before Saturday.'

Brant merely smiled at her and turned to shake Uncle Viv's hand. 'Look after yourself, Viv. It might be an idea if you let Doc Edmonds have a look at that leg.'

'What's wrong with his leg?' Lori's clear, musical voice rose sharply.

'Nothing much, darling. Don't you worry about it.'

'What a silly thing to say!' Lori broke off and stared purposefully into Brant's dark face. 'How do you know about this?'

'Viv just told me. Doc Edmonds still does the rounds. Get him out. It's probably nothing and he'll put your mind at rest.'

A new worry stood clearly in Lori's amber eyes. 'Do you suppose it's anything to do with that old injury when Smoky kicked you?'

'Branded me, you mean!' Uncle Viv said and laughed. 'What a disgraceful thing that was, and I've worked all my life with horses!'

Dianne was pushing her long blonde hair back carefully, standing beside the big estate car as though she was bored. 'Those pawpaws look perfect, Brant!'

'Which reminds me, they're actually for you.' He walked to the rear of the station wagon and opened up the tail gate 'Lori, be a good girl and drape this over the front seat.' He transferred the wall hanging to her waiting arms and lifted the box of tropical fruit out, pawpaws, pineapples and avocados, while Dianne exlaimed over them and walked back with him as he left them in the shade of the veranda.

Lori finished what she was doing and looked back at her uncle. Always a spare man, his thinness seemed more pronounced than ever and his thick grey hair had gone almost white.

'Why didn't you tell me your leg was bothering you?' she demanded.

'It's nothing, Lori. Don't worry, I'm in good health!'

'You told Brant!' she complained.

'Brant's a good listener. Besides, he's another man.'

'Well, I'm going to make you see Doctor Edmonds. Let him be as tough as a bulldog with you. You won't listen to me.'

'Make a nice couple, don't they?' Uncle Viv asked almost tranquilly.

Lori looked towards the deep shaded veranda where Brant and Dianne were still talking, Dianne with her slender arms draped around one vine-wreathed white wooden support. 'Just about the handsomest couple I've ever seen!'

Uncle Viv missed the irony. 'I do so wish Dianne would come home and settle down. At her age, she should be married.'

'Heavens, she's only twenty-five!'

'All the same, it's time she married and had a family. She's as thin as a skeleton with that modelling!'

'Some skeleton!' Lori said in a wry voice.

Uncle Viv's faded brown eyes didn't leave the couple and it was obvious to Lori what he was thinking. Dianne had claimed she knew instantly that Brant was the man for her. Maybe she was right. Brant would know how to keep any woman in line—even Dianne, who would make a rather ruthless adversary. Lori stood and looked at them in silence, feeling a strange premonition.

Rex, her favourite big cattle dog, fresh from a swim in the creek, raced around the side of the house, saw her, and began to welcome her home with his usual exuberance. Lori bent over to pat him, speaking to him more sternly than usual to quieten him. Dianne didn't like dogs and she found Rex and his loud barking quite painful. As it was she was coming towards Lori, frowning.

'Can't you get rid of that monstrous creature? And don't go letting him in the house. I'm allergic to animal hair!'

Rex, so brave when he was working, actually cowered and Brant slapped his knee. 'Here, boy! Want a ride down to the front gate?'

'Not in your good car!' Dianne looked doubtfully at him.

But Rex had heard and was shaking with pleasure. After the ride he usually raced Brant's car along the boundary fence. It was all good fun and when Brant opened the rear door he leapt in looking so sweet and intelligent Lori put her hand in and patted him. 'Don't forget to come home again!'

'Well, to get to work!' Brant slid into the driver's seat and switched on the ignition. They moved away while he backed, then they stood in a little tight group waving.

'No one but you, Lori, would think of introducing that silly creature. I just hope he eats all the tassels off your wall hanging!' Dianne said condemningly.

'How hilarious!'

'You don't suppose he will?' Uncle Viv looked at her anxiously. 'He's made a wreck of a few things in his time.'

'Brant won't let him. Rex knows who he's dealing with!'

'What I don't understand is how Brant came to be interested in such an obvious bit of junk,' said Dianne nastily. 'I mean, these little arts and crafts are all very well for the farm, but his house is full of beautiful things!'

'What a comfort it is, then, to know he's going to hang something of mine!'

'I couldn't be more surprised!' Dianne persisted.

'That's obvious. Let's go inside. If you feel up to it, Uncle Viv, we'd better talk a little business. Mr Sommerville had a few things to say that you'll have to hear.'

'Why don't you just sell out to Brant?' Dianne said coldly. 'It's a colossal mistake letting Lori handle anything, Dad.'

'I'll let you into a little secret, Di,' he said quietly. 'Lori isn't just a hard worker, she has a definite flair for business. McClarry at the bank told me, so did old Sommerville. Bad seasons and my own bad management have ruined us. I miss your mother sorely, in every possible way. She ran the place anyway, and it didn't even strike me until after she was gone. Lori can't do the impossible and she's such a gallant little slip of a thing she makes my heart ache. You two girls must stick together. You're cousins and you're everything I've got in this world.'

Despite her self-centred nature Dianne was moved to slip her hand through her father's and he clasped it as if it were a lifeline. 'I can't tell you too often how wonderful it is to have you home!'

'I really feel I was meant to!' she said with shining confidence. 'All I need now is a new dress for the Brant party. I haven't a darn thing to wear!' Dianne's dark eyes were glittering with excitement and as they walked back up to the house she even began to hum a gay little tune when her thoughts were really erotic. She was thinking of Brant Elliot and her senses were clamouring.

CHAPTER TWO

BRANT sent the men over next day just as he promised, and although Uncle Viv complained often that the 'blasted heat was throttling him' he rode round with Lori for most of the day, expansive over billy tea and a knock-up lunch for the men, but visibly tiring towards mid-afternoon. Albie too kept close to them, Uncle Viv's permanent help, and he took the opportunity of helping out fix the front gate and several panels of fencing. Albie was a long, lean, taciturn individual and the best hand they could manage. If he needed a good shaking up occasionally both Lori and her uncle knew he could be trusted, and he had the hang of working cattle.

'Tracks here where the cattle are gettin' through, boss!' he announced.

'I should think so!' Uncle Viv growled. 'The bloody fence has been down in six places!'

'Can't do everythin', boss. I keep tellin' ya!'

'It's all right, now, Albie,' Lori reassured him. 'Mr Elliott said he'd send a man around the fence.'

'Terrific bloke, that feller!' Albie looked at the ground.

'I'll tell him next time I see him.'

'You look tired, boss?' Albie looked up at the older man, slumped in the saddle.

'I've never liked the idea of riding round in the heat. All a waste of good time anyway. For two pins I'd sell out today.'

'Don't be in too much of a hurry!' Albie cautioned,

no doubt thinking about his own job.

Lori pushed her wide-brimmed hat back off her head and let it hang by the strap. 'Is your leg troubling you, dear?'

'Unfortunately, yes!'

'Then Albie will ride back with you. I'll wait until the men are off the property. I might as well tell you I've made an appointment with Doctor Edmonds. We'll have to drive into the surgery. He wants to give you a thorough check-up.'

'Why old Edmonds?' Uncle Viv said irritably. 'He likes to make a fuss about everything.'

'That's not true. He's the most easygoing man I've ever known, and a very good doctor.'

'Of course he is, and very generous with his time. Didn't he stay with us all the time your aunt was ill?'

Lori's smile was a little sad. 'Then you'll go?'

'I never like going into town,' confessed Uncle Viv. 'Used to love it in the old days.'

'I'll come with you, boss,' Albie offered. 'We'll have a few drinks to take our minds off our troubles!'

'I told you Albie, if you ever go into a pub again I'd bang your ears together!'

Lori couldn't help laughing and Albie's long face coloured with long-remembered shame. 'I give you my solemn oath I'll *never* go wild again. After all, that was three years ago.'

'And you mustn't let the drink get you again!'

'Surely he can enjoy one or two?' Lori put in.

'Keep out of this, Lori!' Uncle Viv said sternly. 'You weren't there.'

Albie lifted himself on to his horse and whistled up the dogs. They came running eagerly as though they were about to tame a wild herd, then stood panting in anticipation.

'Gawd!' said Albie, 'that Rex is gettin' a big feller. Over-eager too. I guess he wants a bit o' work!'

'There's no sense in being boisterous in the heat. Come on, Albie, we'll go back. This leg is giving me gyp!'

Albie glanced at Lori with his mild, colourless eyes. 'Sure you can manage, Miss Lori?'

'In my element, Albie!' she assured him.

'Sure are competent for one small young lady!'

'Are you coming, Albie?' Uncle Viv shouted testily.

'That's right!' Albie nodded back to the boss gravely, then whispered to Lori, ''Course he's tired. A good thing you're gettin' 'im to the doc.'

'I won't be satisfied until I do,' said Lori. 'Go with him now, Albie. I'll be all right!

'Why don't you come with us?' Uncle Viv called to her. 'They're doing a good job!'

Lori's amber eyes were shining. 'This is the time of day I like best. The worst of the heat is nearly over. Give me another hour or so!'

Both men waved and Rex stood uncertainly as if he didn't know which party to follow, but evidently Albie swore at him because he fell into a brisk running trot beside the female, Tory. The day was cooler now and Lori turned her mare's handsome head around. There was still no sign of rain, but at least the falling temperature would lower the fire risk. They needed a deluge anyway. The sun glinted on the scorched grass and the gums turned their drooping green-grey foliage edge-on to the dazzling light. An eye-catching king parrot shot out of a paperbark and flew so low Lori had to duck down over the mare's neck, and further back in the bush she could still hear the saw buzzing. In lots of ways having Brant Elliot for a neighbour was a decided asset.

Lori took the mare at a fast canter down to the front gate. All the rails were up and the sagging hinges mended. It was useless to feel aggrieved that she couldn't have done it herself and it was useless to push Albie. She would have to thank Brant as amiably as she could and ignore the pitying contempt in his blue-green eyes. The parched grass around the bottom of the fence had also been cleared in case it flared into an uncontrollable blaze. It was heartbreaking to have to wait for the rain, and daily their cattle were growing weaker, crowding in round the Pink Lily lagoon and the creek. Every morning the sun rose and raged and in the evening it set in a violent red disc. Lori rode along the fence, her expression intense. Soon the first of the cattle would be dying. It was right to feel alarm, yet from the expression on Uncle Viv's thin, set face he clearly felt there was nothing more he could do.

The sound of a vehicle approaching made her straighten in the saddle and lift her head. It took a little while to come into sight and she recognised Dean's little red runabout. Just at that moment Lori didn't know if she was pleased to see him or not, but at least it wasn't Brant. She dreaded his visits as much as they excited her—there, she had admitted it! But Brant would never be allowed to know. She rode back along the fence and opened the gate so Dean could park his car in the shade, then she slipped off the mare's back and left her standing philosophically under a tamarind tree.

Dean's hair in the sun had the same golden glint as Dianne's. He was a tall, slim young man with deeply shadowed blue eyes that quite often looked tortured. Right now they were smiling, vaguely hungry, and Lori stood quite still, not moving at all.

'I say, that isn't much of a way to greet me!' He

covered the short distance between them and looked deeply into her eyes. 'Hi, I've missed you!'

'You mustn't let yourself miss me,' she said.

'I'm trying not to, but it won't work.'

Lori shook her head and moved back into the shade. 'Come and sit down—or would you like to go up to the house?'

'No, it's you I want to see.' Dean walked a few paces back with her and sank on to the faded grass, pulling her down beside him. 'Take that ancient old hat off, I want to see your face and your hair.'

Lori caught her lower lip between her teeth, but she did as he said. 'Have you started practising again?' she asked.

'Not seriously. I've come home to rest. Mother sits and fumes silently, but so far she hasn't pushed me. Sometimes I feel I've had more than I can take.'

'I would have thought to play the piano as you do would be a wonderful sustaining pleasure.'

'Maybe I'm a fool!' he said bitterly. 'Maybe I didn't deserve the gift at all. Mother had enormous talent, you know, but she never had the opportunities. Granddad was just a dyed-in-the-wool chauvinist not willing to let a woman do anything. He had the money, you know, but he refused to take her talent seriously. I've been tied to a grand piano ever since I can remember, so do you mind not talking about it for a moment!'

Lori sighed and lay back on the grass. 'I don't want to hurt you, Dean. Maybe it's cruel to push a child into a mould!'

Dean turned and let his eyes drop over her sweetly curving body. 'What else could I do? Playing the piano is the only blasted thing I *can* do. Which brings me to what I came over to talk about. I had a call from the Big Man, and I'm still quivering. It seems he wants Mother and me to come along to his party.'

'I think you'd survive it!' Lori said lightly. 'It may even do you good. You're too much on your own.'

Dean had his eyes fixed very penetratingly on her mouth. 'He just happened to mention in passing that you and Di would be going. Is it true?'

'For reasons not very clear to me, yes, I have been invited. Di's inclusion, of course, was inevitable. After all, there aren't that many beautiful girls around.'

'Just between the two of us,' Dean said bluntly, 'I think you leave Dianne for dead!'

'Why, thanks!' Lori returned faintly. 'It's not everyone's opinion.'

'Just ask a man!' Dean returned obscurely. 'What do you really think of Elliot?'

Lori continued to look up at the radiant blue sky. 'I can't disapprove of him too much. He's been very good to us.'

'But surely that's in his own interest. It's no secret he wants the farm.'

'Well, that's a bit tricky,' Lori said stiffly. 'He can't have it!'

Seeing her rising anger, Dean changed the subject. 'He didn't say, but I suppose he'll expect me to play.'

'I'm sure he won't press you, but I'd love to see you give a good account of yourself. Remember I've always been one of your most fervent admirers. How is your mother?' she added politely.

'Who knows how Mother is? She lives all alone—I mean really alone. The only reason she takes any notice of me at all is because I can play.'

Lori turned her head to stare up at him. 'Why don't you cut out on your own?'

'Darling!' Dean almost seemed to hold his breath

for a moment. 'After all Mother's done? I couldn't be so cruel!'

'In my opinion that's foolish. I'm not suggesting you don't see your mother often, but it's about time you led a life of your own.'

Dean reached out a hand and touched her face. 'I could do anything for a woman like you. Everything I am, I'd like to offer you. You're so warm and live and your mouth is exquisite. Let me kiss you, Lori!'

His strong lean hand felt heavy on her face. She wanted to be kind to him and she was moved by the sincerity in his voice. 'Just once!' she said, almost afraid to pull away. There was something about the blueness of his eyes. There was no reality about it for Lori, only a sense of surrender and a quality of empathy. He slipped his hand gently under her chin, his golden head sinking towards hers. A little experience was necessary, but Lori felt no impulse to draw his head down to hers. Her eyelids fluttered and shut, and it was then a hard, mocking voice drenched them in coldness.

'Well now ... I hope I'm not interrupting?'

The arm that supported Dean trembled violently and in the next second he had jumped to his feet. 'For a big man you certainly move silently!' he snapped.

'Actually I gave a little gasp when I saw you, but obviously you didn't hear. Don't worry, I know all about young love!'

Lori blinked and went to push up, but Brant reached down and very nearly jerked her to her feet. 'Sorry if I startled you. I came over across the creek. The men have done a remarkably good job.' The brilliant aquamarine gaze fastened on the slipped button on her shirt and she had an irresistible urge to hit him, but she couldn't summon up the strength.

Dean, too, seemed in a daze. 'I wanted to speak to Lori about the party,' he explained.

'And I'm very pleased both of you are coming!' Brant said in a remarkably pleasant voice. 'Naturally we won't press you, but I'm sure we'd all be delighted to hear you play. Lori has prepared me for a treat.'

Go on, snub him! Lori thought violently, but Dean, too, seemed determined to be affable. 'I've any number of party pieces in the repertoire so it shouldn't be any problem,' he told Brant.

'Good, then that's settled!'

Lori could feel her antagonism showing in her face. Her great amber eyes even caught the same gleaming fire as her hair. 'Sorry to rock the boat, but I simply can't promise anything at the moment.'

'Oh, don't be tiresome, Lori!' Brant admonished her. 'Dean is depending on you for support.'

'For God's sake, *yes*!' Dean turned a little desperately towards her as though he was about to be trapped.

'What a contrary little wretch you are, Lori!' Brant said conversationally.

'You should certainly know!' she said shortly. 'Is there any reason why you wanted to speak to me?'

His eyes changed abruptly to a definite green and he looked frankly dangerous. 'Arrogant little bitch!'

'She isn't usually!' Dean stressed, his blue eyes full of concern. 'Look here, I'd better go. I just wanted to make sure Lori was coming to the party. With all due respect, Mr Elliot, it will make a big difference to me.'

'Brant, please!' the older man invited. 'I don't like to cut your conversation short, but there are one or two things I'd like to warn Lori in advance about.'

'Such as?'

'A few things I'd expect you to see!' His eyes narrowed to slits and the line of his jaw hardened. 'Among other things I'd shift the cattle away from the Pink Lily lagoon. It looks like turning into a bog!'

'I'd better take myself off,' Dean murmured diplomatically. 'In any case, Mother's expecting me.'

'Please give her my regards,' Brant said suavely, and even turned to walk with Dean to the car.

Lori stood still for a moment clenching her fists, then she hurried after them. 'If you've got nothing better to do tomorrow, Dean, let's take a run into the Junction, after lunch.'

'I couldn't think of anything I'd like better!' Dean turned to smile at her. 'I'll pick you up, shall I?'

'Fine!' She waited until he was seated, then on a mad impulse she leant through the window and kissed his cheek. 'Listen, you'll probably want to play something else, but I like the Ritual Fire Dance!'

'You would!' Brant breathed behind her, but Dean looked pleased.

'The Ritual Fire Dance it is. I should be able to manage it with practice or not!'

'Nice to see you!' Brant added suavely, and took Lori's arm, drawing her away from the car.

Dean spun it around in a semicircle, then he took off in a cloud of dust, honking the horn and waving when he was through the gate.

'What's got into him?' Brant asked.

'What the devil do you mean?'

'I understood he suffered from depression.'

She ignored the hard mocking light in his eyes. 'Not today!'

'That was fairly obvious. Don't go looking for trouble, young Lori. There might be other days he's not quite so agreeable. He strikes me as being altogether too intense.'

'You don't know him!' She flickered a glance at his cleft chin and away again. 'I might very well take it into my head to be the little woman in the background.'

'And that says it!' he agreed. 'Pity he didn't have any brothers and sisters.'

'I shouldn't say this, Brant, but I hate you!' she ground out.

'I do believe you do!' he said drily. 'Well, good for you. I'm not looking for your girlish affection!'

'You get a lot of exercise, don't you, cutting me down to size?' Lori snapped.

'There's really no need to, you don't even come up to my shoulder!' He studied her in silence for a moment with his glittery gaze. 'How many times have you let Stanton kiss you?'

'A round robin of embraces!' she returned sweetly. 'He does it all the time.'

'The hell he does! No one yet has kissed you properly.'

'Why haven't you, with your cold-blooded ego?' she demanded.

'Because, little one, it would be a disaster!'

If she didn't actually hate him she came very close. He was such a cynical brute with a cruel sense of humour. She didn't know it, but her small face was charging with all her emotions and her amber eyes were eloquent of her undisciplined rage.

'You're asking too much of me, do you know that?' Brant said lightly. 'I suppose I could kiss you or turn you over my knee. I must add that the last one has the more appeal!'

'What about the money you owe me?'

'How unladylike to think of it!' He smiled and it lit his dark face. 'Anything is preferable to disappointing you. I have it with me, as a matter of fact.' He reached into his breast pocket and withdrew a wad of notes. 'What do you say?'

'Thank you!'

'Nothing else?'

'Not even if my life depended upon it!'

'I suppose I'll hardly recognise you in a dress!' he mused.

'Oh, you *beast*!' she said despairingly. 'As a matter of fact I'm going to make it out of something that shimmers.'

'Make it yellow,' he suggested.

'I thought pink!' she said flippantly, and he reached out and tweaked a red-gold strand.

'You couldn't afford it!'

'Anyway, Dean has excellent taste. He can help me.'

'I'll bet!' He reached the mare first and swung into the saddle. 'Come on up!'

'I prefer to walk!'

For answer he seized her and she looked up frantically. 'All right. You'll crack my ribs!'

He took her up before him and she clung to him convulsively for a second. 'You do the most unexpected things!' she gasped.

'I don't know!' he said drily. 'I've resisted some powerful urges in my time.' His arm encircled her slight body and drew her back against him. 'Lori, relax! Anyone would think I was the Lord of the Underworld making off with you.'

'What a terrible situation!'

'And with one so much younger than myself!'

Impulsively she did relax so they flowed together with the horse. When they arrived back at the section of scrub the men were clearing her honey-coloured skin was flushed with colour and she looked very young and full of a dancing vitality. The men had gone, but a four-wheel-drive stood in the clearing.

As Brant dismounted his hand slid up under her breast and it gave her such a fluttering, breathless feeling she was momentarily overcome. She had never, ever, been so close to him before and the effect was absolutely stunning. She veiled her eyes with her long lashes so he couldn't see her bewildered inexperience and he put up his hands and lifted her down off the mare.

'Just what, by the way, are you thinking?' he asked.

'That yellow is the wrong colour.'

He left his hands on either side of her narrow waist the tips of his fingers touching her hipbones. 'Yellow could be a colour especially designed for you. You'll look stunning, like a sunflower.'

'Maybe I want to look like a lily!'

'Then you'll have to wear a hat!' He stood smiling down at her with a faintly quizzical look. 'I find this most unusual to have you still beneath my hands!'

'I have the feeling one false move and I'll get crushed!'

'And you're afraid!'

'I think I should be, don't you?' She looked up suddenly and caught his expression. He looked so dominant, so damned sure of himself, she brought up her own hands and pushed his away. 'It's getting late!'

'I know that!' he said as though humouring her. 'Why you haven't done up that button on your blouse I don't know. Or did Stanton undo it?'

'Of course not!' She flashed a disgusted look at him and the colour rushed under the pale gold of her skin.

'Don't dither!'

Her fingers were shaking and he slipped the smooth pearly disc through the button hole. 'You've changed a lot in the last four years.'

'Oh, *shut up*!' she snapped.

'Don't worry, I like it. If you were a little older and wiser there'd be fireworks!'

'Even then I'd play it smart and stick with my own league. Thanks for what you did for us today,' she added. 'It's a pleasure to see the fence up. If I were a man...'

'Oh, Lori!' Brant drawled meaningly, and slid into the driver's seat of the jeep. 'I know it's hard to get Albie's attention, but get him to shift the cattle round and don't have the dogs snapping at their heels. The water level in the lagoon has fallen considerably. They're too indolent in the heat and they'll get bogged.'

'I'll tell him,' she said awkardly, embarrassed on Uncle Viv's account.

'Get him to walk them to some shade first thing in the morning,' Brant added.

'Right, boss!' She touched her blazing hair.

Brant smiled a little grimly as though it was impossible not to admire her spirit even if the whole situation was infuriating, then with a: 'So long, little one!' he switched on the ignition and put the jeep into gear.

Lori stood watching until he had disappeared through the trees making for the creek crossing both properties shared. Oh, for just a little of Brant's money! She'd hire extra staff and buy extra feed and sit out the drought. Mr Sommerville had made the point over and over that Uncle Viv had made no provision for lean times and their bank overdraft was past an acceptable limit. Why didn't Uncle Viv see Mr

Sommerville himself? The answer was simple: Uncle Viv was a sick man. Lori had no doubt either that she would have trouble getting him in to Doctor Edmonds, the only thing in her favour was, Dianne might consent to accompany them. Every day of her life now Lori wondered how Aunt Jocelyn had ever come to have such a daughter.

By lunchtime the next day, Lori was so tired she regretted having arranged the trip into the Junction. She and Albie had been up since first light bringing the weakest of the cows and the calves into the ironbox country close to a permanent waterhole. Two of the calves had lost their mothers and their pitiful bellowing was still ringing in her ears. It should never have happened. More, it seemed irresponsible. Albie, too, had had a bad morning when his faithful old Jess put her foot in a melon hole and horse and rider came crashing down. The swearing had been something to hear, carrying vibrantly on the dry radiant air, but Lori had been too worried about both of them to take much offence. At any rate, it had the desired effect on Jess, for she was on her feet almost immediately with Albie, the sloppiest horseman around, belatedly apologising. Albie's exhibitions of swearing were almost as spectacular as his drinking and whip-cracking, but although the swearing was extremely colourful, Lori never found it profane, possibly because she had long since tuned out.

By the time they rode in for lunch, they were both speechless and soaked in sweat, dog-tired and irritable. They had needed at least two others to help them, but Uncle Viv had been deaf to staff problems for a long time. Albie, who liked to eat alone, went off mumbling and Lori dragged herself up the front stairs with the vague intention of ringing Dean and cancelling their outing. If the heat had not killed her hunger she would have been further distressed to know there was no lunch waiting for her, but at least Dianne had found it in her heart to make a cup of tea and some sandwiches for her father.

Uncle Viv was sitting in his favourite planter's chair out on the veranda and his bushy eyebrows drew together as he saw Lori's small, weary figure.

'Where did you shift them to?' he asked.

'Close in, near the waterhole. Two of the calves have lost their mothers. They were so damned miserable!'

'I never like the idea of your doing this kind of work,' Uncle Viv said with difficulty.

'It had to be done straight away!' Lori tried to speak cheerily. 'You'll have to excuse me, darling, I must shower and change. Dean is giving me a lift into the Junction this afternoon.'

'Is he picking you up here?'

'Yes.' Lori looked at the half-eaten pile of sandwiches. 'Di got your lunch—that's good.'

Uncle Viv drew in a long breath of regret. 'It's not much fun for her. She's lying down at the moment. She doesn't tolerate the heat as well as you do,'

Lori was about to add something colourful of her own, but she changed her mind at the last minute, seeing the stiff mask of pain on Uncle Viv's face. 'How are you feeling?' she asked anxiously.

'All right!' he returned shortly, and loosened his clenched fingers. 'All right, dear, don't worry!'

'Can you see me not worrying about you?' she asked gently. 'Your appointment is Friday morning. Maybe I should have insisted he take you right away.'

'Look, dear, I told you,' Uncle Viv narrowed his

eyes against the light, 'I'm all right!' He put out his hand and Lori put her own into it.

'Poor old Albie took a fall,' she said humorously, and had the satisfaction of seeing Uncle Viv's face relax.

'I bet the air turned blue as usual!'

'Well, he's never light-on with the bloodies!' She laughed a little, then spoke more seriously. 'We really need a few spare horses.'

'Yes!' Uncle Viv agreed, and then more irritably, 'Di might be right about selling out. It seems obvious that's what we'll have to do!'

Lori turned round and looked out on the property she loved. No true countrywoman could resist the fascination of the wide open spaces. Despite the drought, the poor condition of the cattle, the falling market, Uncle Viv's loss of belief in himself, she wanted desperately to hang on. When the rain came the grass would be long and green and their cattle would be sleek-coated and fat with the good life. Then the parched country would be beautiful again and the lagoons would be full of whistling ducks; entrancingly beautiful, floating their canopies of lilies.

'If we could only stick it out until the rain!' she said softly. 'Drought is ugly, but think of the good times. We'll get a good season and this will turn into the Promised Land again. If Brant can make such a wonderful success of everything so can we. Just give us some rain and we'll recover. The cattle will fill their bellies with good grass and we won't know them!'

'Even then our troubles wouldn't be over!' Uncle Viv looked out at the vivid blue sky, pitiless and majestic. 'Anyway, there doesn't seem much likelihood of even a drop, not even a thunderstorm. The whole countryside is ready to go up in a blaze and all we can talk about is when the rain's coming. It's not coming, Lori, not for a good while. I'll have to shoot Tilly. She's turning into a tottering old wreck.'

'No, she looks better!' Lori swung around and faced her uncle defiantly. 'I've been hand-feeding her. You can't shoot Tilly. I'm too fond of her—and anyway, she thinks she's human. You couldn't go out and shoot an old lady!'

'Maybe not. You're the expert. Just keep your eye on her. You're doing a man's job, do you know that?'

'As Albie would say,' she said lightly, 'I earn me tucker!'

'Never mind Albie!' Uncle Viv returned rather hotly. 'He gets paid. *You* don't!'

Lori kept her voice even. 'And of course I wasn't reared and looked after lovingly all these long years?'

'Sh-sh!' Uncle Viv leaned forward and patted her. 'Don't talk about that. Your aunt wouldn't like to see you soaked in sweat like you are now. It must have been hell out there in the sun!' A faint spasm crossed his eyes and forehead. 'It's too vast for you, Lori, and all Albie's good for is yelling his head off. I'm terribly sorry to say it, but I can't help you much these days. Go in, dear, and get ready. If you want to stay out to tea, do so. We can manage here. You deserve a little time for relaxation. You work too hard, but I have no one to take your place!'

Dispiritedly, Uncle Viv closed his eyes and Lori pressed a hand to his shoulder then went into the house. It was a critical time for the farm, but she wasn't prepared to surrender all the time and the effort they had put into it, all the hard work Aunt Jocelyn had done.

Brant planned to extend his cottonfields and she

realised he was becoming so successful he had to, but he would have to swing wide of the farm. No one in their right senses would fight him, but she knew exactly that that was what she intended to do. If they only had the capital and the knowhow, they could go into cotton themselves, with the beef market depressed. If only she was a man she could undo more easily this seemingly hopeless tangle. It was no use trying to spur Uncle Viv on; he hadn't the heart or the health. Maybe, as Brant had pointed out to her, she would finish with very little to show for herself. Uncle Viv adored Dianne, his only child, and naturally she would be heiress to everything he possessed.

Overheated, Lori ran a cold shower and shampooed her hair all in the space of ten minutes. Later when she was dressing in her bedroom, Dianne, who scorned knocking, walked in.

'God, isn't it hot!' she said in an agonised voice, and curled herself languidly into an armchair. 'It's all so damned primitive here!'

'You have the fan!' Lori pointed out rather acidly.

'And isn't it a blessing!' Dianne darted a quick look at the younger girl. 'You're quite clever with the needle, aren't you?'

'I thought you'd never notice! It's easy to sew when one has to.'

'Yes, I suppose it would be useful. I couldn't bear to wear anything home-made myself.'

Lori flicked the brush through her hair and glanced at her cousin's face reflected in the mirror. She probably was feeling the heat, for she looked rather pale. 'What are you wearing Saturday night?' she asked.

Dianne contemplated her beautiful long nails. 'People always expect me to look marvellous. It gets a bit wearing at times!'

'Nothing's free!' Lori returned blithely. 'Even being beautiful!'

'Well,' Dianne hesitated, unexpectedly mollified, 'I thought the silver caftan?'

'It should be sensational!'

'And while you're in town, make an appointment for me at the hairdressers. Saturday morning would be best. My hair has suffered dreadful damage just in the few weeks I've been here.'

'But you do give it lots of protection!'

'Which is more than one can say for you!' Dianne flicked a glance over Lori's soft red-gold locks. 'Why don't you see if they can do something to tone down your hair? You're not bad looking, but you really should get something to cover those freckles.'

'Anything else?' Lori asked lightly, 'You're giving me an inferiority complex.'

'Well, you're not very ambitious, dear, are you? Dean mightn't be the man to send me delirious, but you could land him if you tried!'

'Dean's just a friend!' Lori said firmly. 'We've known him all our lives.'

'That's not sensible!' Dianne said disapprovingly. 'There's not very much offering around here and if he could get rid of his dreadful mother he may very well continue to ornament the concert world. A girl needs a meal ticket, and he's madly in love with you. Why don't you take pity on him?'

'Hmm!' Lori murmured noncommittally, and hunted up her shopping bag.

'Why do you always change the subject when I suggest something sensible!' Dianne asked in disgust.

'Surely you've noticed I don't happen to be in love with Dean.'

'Really, Lori, you're priceless! Surely you don't

expect some shining knight to charge up here?'

'It *can* happen!' Lori smiled rather twistedly and Dianne's dark almond eyes narrowed.

'I don't normally pay much attention to gossip, but I've heard a few funny things about you tossing yourself at Brant.'

'Then forget them!' Lori murmured. 'They were all lies!' She stood in the middle of the room, a small very slender girl whose amber eyes showed her fatigue. 'Is there anything you'd like me to get you? I may be back late.'

Dianne stood up so suddenly she nearly lost her footing. 'Aren't you going to get dinner? I've asked Gavin over.'

'You might have told me!' said Lori crossly.

'I'm telling you now, aren't I?' Dianne replied arrogantly. 'Dad is always telling me what a good little cook you are, not that I've really fallen for it, but you're certainly better than I am. I counted on your being here!'

Lori studied her cousin's beautiful chiselled face, the tall, slender, perfectly proportioned body. Even in a broderie anglaise camisole and shorts she looked very much the professional model, and her long, loosely falling hair was fairer than it had been when she was a child. 'Forgive my mentioning it,' Lori said drily, 'but you'll have to help out with the money. My budget doesn't run to chicken and champagne!'

Dianne's porcelain skin flushed. 'Why don't you ask Dad?'

'I'm not going to. He has enough on his plate at the moment. The farm isn't paying, Di. You know that.'

'How you endure it at all, I don't know! All right, I'll get some from my room. Don't make a habit of asking, because I won't give it to you. There's no whisky around either,' Dianne added. 'You might get another bottle.'

'Leave it to me!' Lori's amber eyes had a strange expression. 'If you don't mind I'll bring Dean back as well. I have an idea he was going to ask me to eat in town.'

'Please yourself!' Dianne gave an elegant shrug. 'I hope you'll be back in plenty of time. It's so *embarrassing* the way we live!'

'We've lived pretty well up until now,' Lori pointed out shortly. 'There happens to be a drought on!'

As was her way, Dianne ignored her. 'I can't wait until Saturday. I wonder what Brant's relatives will be like? At least they'll be waited on hand and foot. Even in these supposedly hard times Brant lives like a prince!'

Lori was on the point of cheering, but she heard the dogs start up their barking outside. Dean must have arrived. Probably Brant had invited them up to the house out of sheer pity, but she couldn't say that to Dianne, who had developed a deliberate passion for him. Dianne needed a man who could lavish every material possession on her, otherwise he couldn't be considered. Gavin's family also happened to have money, and Gavin was grateful for Dianne's least little glance.

Dianne walked out of the room in silence and Lori gathered up her things and followed her. It was odd how unready Dianne was to help out with her father in financial difficulties. Dianne came back with a crisp note, and Lori looked down at it and thanked her. 'Chicken suit you?'

'Yes, and look here, I'd like a nice sweet!'

'I could make a pineapple pavlova or a strawberry mousse,' Lori offered. 'You'd save me a few minutes if you'd set the table and pick some passionfruit off the vines.'

'I guess I can do that!' Dianne drawled. 'Have a lovely time!'

Lori tucked the twenty-dollar bill into her purse and looked back to her cousin. 'Why don't you get out the silver candelabra?'

'Good idea!'

'They'll probably need cleaning.'

Dianne scowled and declined the effort. 'I don't want to break my nails. Not before Saturday!'

'Ah well, get them out anyway. You'll look most effective by candlelight and I'll be back in time. Use the beige lace tablecloth and the red linen napkins. They're in the sideboard. Now I must go!'

Outside in the sunlight Lori nearly came to an abrupt stop. The very fact that Uncle Viv had disappeared should have prepared her. Dean had brought along his mother and she sat, stiff-backed and handsome, in the bucket seat beside him. For a moment Lori was so numb she couldn't feel anything. It had started off a dreadful day and it certainly wasn't improving.

Dean swung out of the small car and looked over the top of it winningly. 'How early am I?'

'Right on time!'

'I brought Mother,' he said, and looked back into the car brightly. 'Not too hot for you, is it, darling?'

Whatever Mrs Stanton replied Lori didn't hear. She walked on to the car and slipped into the back seat without Dean's help. 'How are you, Mrs Stanton?'

'No less hot and bothered than we all are!' Mrs Stanton replied charmingly, and cast her cold blue eyes over as much of Lori as she could see. 'I should think you'd burn with no sleeves in your dress, Lori?'

'Not really!' Lori murmured apologetically. 'I have an even tan.'

'I wish I had one!' Dean said mechanically, as though his mother's presence reduced him to all kinds of banalities.

A touch of exasperation touched his mother's face. 'I don't doubt we're ready to go, Dean!'

Dean leaned forward, hunched up his long legs and re-started the car. 'I haven't seen much of Di.'

'Well, actually she wants you to come to dinner to-night. Gavin Camfield is coming as well.'

'I thought she'd have him tucked away somewhere. Poor old Gavin, he had his heart set on Di in the first grade!'

'Do us a favour, dear, and keep up on the track!' his mother muttered, narrowing her eyes for a moment against the rising dust.

'Sorry, darling!' Dean returned automatically, with a kind of little-boy-forlorn grace. He looked very neat and clean and his blond hair was shining.

Mrs Stanton cast her eyes expertly around the property and it seemed to Lori she looked positively horrified. 'I dare not ask how things are!' she commented at last.

'We've survived droughts before,' Lori said mildly, and hoped Mrs Stanton would take the hint.

'I'm afraid this time you haven't got your aunt!' Mrs Stanton continued most joltingly. 'I expect Viv feels quite hopeless without her.'

'He misses her, yes. We all do.' Lori began to wonder just how much of Mrs Stanton she could take.

'And what brings Dianne back home?' she asked with a small inquiring smile.

'To see her father, of course!' Lori returned swiftly.

'You two girls never were close,' pursued Mrs Stanton. 'Of course, Dianne was always the pretty one and you were so small, with that *splitting* red hair!'

Dean had been looking straight in front of him, but now he glanced at his mother, looking incongruously like her. 'Really, Mother, I don't know anyone who doesn't admire Lori's hair. Particularly considering she's only got one or two freckles and a beautiful skin!'

Lori found suddenly she could laugh. 'Thanks, Dean. I need someone to make me feel nice!'

'Dean is instinctively kind!' his mother said rather shortly, and Lori was confronted yet again with a disagreeable fact. Mrs Stanton didn't like her, and didn't waste time hiding it. It had been like that ever since Dean had received two black eyes fighting for her one unforgettable afternoon after school. It had been more than six years ago, but apparently some things went deep. Lori sat back trying to look unobtrusive, while Mrs Stanton continued to speak to her son in her well-bred but rather insistent voice. Now and again Dean looked back at Lori in the rear vision, but he was kept fully occupied answering his mother and Lori had the painful suspicion that it would always be so. It was a great pity. Dean Stanton was gifted far above the ordinary, but his mother appeared not to notice it at all.

By the time they reached Junction Lori was almost desperate to get out of the car. Blast Dean for not telling her he was bringing his mother! He really was an idiot sometimes. It occurred to her that once again she might have to take the bus home, otherwise the

return trip might provide some irretrievable catas-
trophe. Whatever she did or said, Mrs Stanton resented it at once, and Lori was well aware that she
really did have the redhead's proverbial quick temper.

Dean assisted his mother out of the car and once
again Lori climbed out unaided. The Stantons were
quite well off, so she often wondered why they ran
such a small car. It was all she could do to dispose of
her own legs in the car's cramped interior, and both of
the Stantons were tall. Just for a moment she had an
amusing vision of Brant suffering such a ride and the
very thought made her smile.

Dean, standing on the pavement, saw the quick
smile and showed his surprise. 'All right, Lori?'

'Yes, thank you!'

Mrs Stanton shook out a fold of her silk skirt and
said condescendingly, 'I suppose you've got lots of
shopping to do, Lori? What time do you think you'll
be through?'

'I've a few things to get for Dianne and I wanted to
get some material for myself. A good hour or so, I
suppose.'

'I hope so, dear!' Mrs Stanton looked inconveni-
enced. 'My own shopping time won't extend so far
and it's dreadfully hot!'

Lori heard herself say rapidly, 'I certainly don't
expect you to wait for me. I can easily catch the bus.'

'Don't be silly!' Dean said with commendable
gallantry. 'We'll wait for you!'

Mrs Stanton's tense expression showed what she
thought of her son's lack of consideration, but she
said coolly enough, 'I suppose we could have a cup of
tea somewhere. Let's arrange a time, shall we?' Across
the street she saw two acquaintances and waved her
strong, narrow hand.

'I'd rather we didn't!' said Lori, and put on her sunglasses. 'I don't like to keep you waiting, and I do have rather a lot to do.'

'Thank you, dear!' Mrs Stanton said composedly. 'Are you coming, Dean? I can't manage by myself!'

Dean leaned towards Lori and said with over-pitched emphasis, 'Well, actually I was thinking of going with Lori. She wanted me to help her decide on material.'

Mrs Stanton paused commandingly. 'You've heard my wishes, Dean. I expect you to respect them. *I've* always put your wishes and interests first and I should like to get our business in the town over. I always fear a migraine in the heat.'

With a kind of detached incredulity Lori heard Dean still protesting that he was going along with her and she leaned back against the car for support. It was a domestic miracle of sorts, Dean defying his mother, but she wanted no part of it. 'Please,' she said, and looked round at both of them, 'don't worry about a thing, either of you. Obviously I've chosen the wrong time to come in with you, but it's hardly a disaster. I'll catch the bus home.'

'I won't hear of it!' said Dean, and his face looked determined and shut.

'Well then, that's quite different, isn't it!' Mrs Stanton looked rather bitterly at her son. 'I'm well aware of the influence Lori has on you, and I've told you before I'm not happy about it!'

Lori straightened up abruptly, appalled beyond words. 'Please don't let's discuss it on the pavement. Go with your mother, Dean. You can see how she feels!'

'In God's name, *why*, Mother?' Dean demanded convulsively.

'Naturally, Dean, I expected you to help me. I'm surprised I should have to point it out to you. I hardly know you in these moods—but I suppose I must learn to cope!' She turned away without looking at Lori, a handsome ageing woman, and a woman of temperament despite her cold manner. The road was clear and she walked quickly across it, heading towards the variety of shops that offered just about anything a person could possibly require.

Dean just stood there with a leaden expression and Lori groaned. 'How terribly upsetting! Honestly, Dean, couldn't you have told me your mother intended coming today?'

'I begin to ask myself now why I didn't. I just keep hoping and hoping you two will hit it off. She can speak pleasantly enough to everyone else. It's you she objects to, and it's dragged on too long. You're a fine girl!'

'I'll say I am!' Lori said wryly. 'I'll even let you go after your mother. I'm sorry she feels the way she does about me, but I'm afraid there's no altering it. Go ahead, Dean. Go after her. She went into Morgan's.'

'Perhaps I'd better!' said Dean, and his voice was dry in his throat. 'She really does suffer dreadfully with migraines.'

'Maybe she fills her head with a whole lot of unpleasant thoughts. Go on, get it over!'

Dean swung about and confronted her, his blue eyes looking strangely tortured again. 'What about you?'

'I told you, I'll catch the bus. I've done it before and I'll do it again.'

'Well, ring me when you get into Bellara. We'll be home by then and I'll come to your rescue. Am I still invited tonight?'

Lori raised her winged eyebrows. 'Do you think you'll be allowed to?'

Dean stared at her silently for a moment. 'Just let me handle it in my own way. Sometimes Mother comes on a bit strong, but...'

'I know, I know!' Lori dismissed his explanation impatiently. 'It's just not my day!' Dean put out his hand to her, but she made a movement of complete withdrawal. 'See you later!'

'Ring me!' Dean called after her, but Lori didn't turn her head. She had no intention of making that phone call. This time Dianne could come in for her if she wanted the dinner prepared. The sun was burning on her back and bare arms and right through her cotton dress, and she headed straight for the coolness of the hairdressing salon to make the appointment for Dianne.

Much later in the afternoon when she looked down the street she saw that Dean's red runabout was no longer in the parking zone. It gave her a sense of freedom to know they were gone. The district had been fascinated for years with the old story of how Dean's father had run off when Dean was a small child and Lori thought, not for the first time, that perhaps he had become terrified of his fate. Mrs Stanton would make anyone nervous and she never missed a chance to reduce her son to an ungrateful small boy. That was what he was, of course—immature—and much as Lori occasionally loathed Brant he was such a vastly different type, his male arrogance in retrospect seemed positively delightful. Brant wasn't the kind to tolerate a woman's domination and he had, of course, warned her about Dean, Big, conceited creature, was he ever wrong?

Anne at the hairdressers looked after her parcels, so

she spent a leisurely, relaxing half hour looking at materials and browsing through patterns, and at last she settled on an extravagantly beautiful piece of material and a very simple style. It was an unexpectedly luxurious feeling to have money in her purse, so she went ahead and splurged on another piece of material to make into a wrap-around skirt. Anne had already talked her into buying some shimmering new make-up, foundation, lipstick and blusher, and having gone that far Lori bought mascara and eyeshadow too. So much drama for one evening, but she had to come to grips with the Raggedy Ann image. She'd make herself so beautiful they'd all come to a halt when they saw her.

It was a brilliantly beautiful late afternoon and a dangerous little breeze had sprung up, making the blossoms drop off the larkspur jacarandas, carpeting the pavements with trumpet-shaped petals. The Junction had the same carefree atmosphere as Bellara but it was much bigger and far more progressive and every time she came in, some new building was going up. Feeling tired now, Lori collected her parcels from Anne, expressed her thanks, and made her way out on to the street again. She had one block to walk to the bus depot, and even that seemed as much as she could possibly manage.

'Where the devil are *you* going?' asked a voice close behind her.

Lori turned around and her eyes deepened and darkened. 'Hi!'

Brant wasn't smiling and he looked bigger than ever. 'Aren't you rather off the track for the parking lot?'

'I'm going down to the bus stop,' she explained.

'You're what?' He swung his hand out and took

charge of her parcels. 'Where the hell's Stanton? You look incredibly frail!'

'I suppose it's the heat or something!' She tried to reassure him, for his dark face was all angles and his blue-green eyes turbulently alive.

'Isn't Stanton with you?' he persisted. 'Mind how you go,' he said sharply, and moved forward and caught her arm. 'You're swaying!'

'It's the breeze.' She tried for self-protection to speak brightly. 'Actually Dean brought me in, but his mother came too!'

'Now it looks as if he's gone! I saw the car earlier and I remembered you'd arranged a little pleasure jaunt. Whose idea was it to bring along a chaperone?'

'That's obvious!' she said, and any more words failed her. She was too tired. The intentness of Brant's regard was frightening her and his manner was, as always, more commanding and expressive than he knew.

'So he went off and left you!' said Brant, over-gently.

'With my assent!' Lori willed her voice to conviction.

'What a loyal little fool you are! Do yourself a favour and break it up now. Stanton will never escape the safe clutches of his mother. Maybe he wants it that way, no matter how much he denies it. Now, I'm going to get you a stiff drink before you pass out.'

'I'm sorry,' said Lori, 'but I don't think I can walk back to the pub!'

'Who's asking you to walk?' he returned bluntly. 'Just sit right down here and I'll bring the car up.'

He compelled her backwards to where a bench circled a dazzling jacaranda and Lori sat down and looked up into his face. 'Don't be long!' At any other time her sense of humour would have made her laugh at such a request of Brant Elliot, but now she was serious. He was so indescribably dependable!

He didn't linger but walked away quickly, and she found herself absently admiring the lithe, co-ordinated movements of his tall, powerful body. Trust Brant to turn up at the psychological moment, even if there was no softening in his hard, handsome face. There was something exquisite about a man's strength, and as she looked down at her small, finely shaped hands with their boyishly clipped nails, she saw they were shaking. Her eyes were enormous, a shimmering amber, and her hair fell over her face like a living shield. A blossom dropped into her lap and she picked it up and examined it with profound admiration. She would have to explain to Brant that she had to be home reasonably early to prepare the dinner. For the first time in her life she really felt like a strong drink, but it would probably affect her, especially since she had had no lunch.

She saw the big station wagon coming up with the traffic, then it slid into a loading zone, braked and turned around when the road was clear. Lori stood up and hurried over to the car. Brant, from the driver's seat, opened out the door and she slid in beside him, seeing her groceries and parcels neatly stacked in the rear compartment.

'Thanks a lot!' she ventured at once.

'My pleasure!' he returned laconically.

'Honestly, Brant, there's no need to buy me a drink. I really have to get home—Di has invited Gavin Camfield over for dinner.'

'So?' he asked tersely.

'So I have to get it, and believe me, it takes time!'

He looked her way briefly. 'How do you explain yourself, Lori?' he demanded.

'Meaning what?'

'You seem bent on sacrificing yourself for others. Let Dianne get the dinner!'

'I asked Dean as well!'

'How strange!' he said in a voice that disturbed her. 'I'd be shocked beyond words if you ever asked *me*!'

She found her voice a little wearily. 'It just never occurred to me that you might want to come.'

'I think I could stand it!' Brant pulled in in front of the very picturesque country hotel and sat for a moment with his hand clenched on the wheel. 'When did you last eat? You seem to be falling away to nothing!'

'Maybe I've lost a few pounds, but I feel O.K.'

'That's not answering my question!' His brilliant eyes were half closed like a cat's and without realising it Lori reacted nervously.

'Let's get out!' She pushed open the door and hurried on ahead, walking through the delicate archway of flowers that led to the two-storied building, its verandas decorated with some wonderful old white cast-iron lace.

Brant caught her up easily, and took her arm, seeing the curious, repressed excitement in her small face. 'You seem to love running away!' he drawled.

'I told you, I haven't got that much time.'

'And you're right about that!' Though his voice was quite matter-of-fact, something in his expression made Lori's heart leap in her breast.

'That sounds vaguely like a threat!'

'Yes!' he said.

They turned right at the entrance and walked through to the lounge. Several people they knew were relaxing over a cold beer and although they all exchanged nods and smiles, Brant steered Lori determinedly towards a quiet corner.

'What will you have?' he asked.

'I think just about anything would put me to sleep.'

'What's wrong with that? You look like a little girl who's been allowed up too long!'

She moistened her mouth with the tip of her tongue and tried to say something, but he clicked his tongue with amused impatience and walked away to the bar, stopping on the way to pass some remark to Lew Taylor, one of the district's biggest graziers. Lew's laugh reached her easily and he turned his head and gave her a humorous little salute that she responded to with a sweet, uncomplicated smile.

After a minute Brant came back with a foaming beer for himself and a long, frosted drink for Lori, complete with crushed ice, a slice of lemon and a sprig of mint.

'What is it?' she asked.

'Just a very mild gin squash.' He sat down and relaxed. 'I can't afford to lose sight of your tender age. Meg will bring along a few sandwiches in a minute. They might take care of a hint of that exhaustion. Your eyes are like saucers!'

'I don't know why you're so good to me!' She gave a husky little laugh.

'First of all, Lori, I feel strongly about a girl having to work so hard, and then I find your spirit and innocence rather touching!' He leaned back and studied her face. 'How you ever got mixed up with Stanton I don't know. As a matter of fact it seems to me he's mildly psychotic.'

'So would you be if you had a mother like that!' retorted Lori.

'My dear child, grow up!' he said forcibly. 'The boy has his freedom and independence for the asking. You've told me he's loaded with gifts, and I happen to know his grandfather was loaded with money and the chief beneficiary was the boy. What's he doing here, suffering from a breakdown, submerging his own will? He should be applying himself. No one is successful without a great deal of hard work, and if he finds the thought of the concert world grim, then he should turn his attention to something else.'

Lori lifted her glass and held it to a gleam of light. 'Not everyone has the fortitude to stand on their own feet. Dean has moments when he's unsure of himself and has to go to someone for help. His mother...'

'Or a wife!' He returned her gaze coolly, and his brilliant eyes glittered without compassion. 'I don't give a damn about his mother, maybe he's compelling her to dominate him, but I do care about you. If I don't tell you you might never know until it's too late!'

'Cheers!' she said, and took a quick sip of her drink. 'That's just what I need, a Big Brother!'

'And what a pity I don't feel particularly brotherly!'

Lori's quick flush betrayed her. She gazed back speechlessly over the rim of the glass at him, blinking her heavy lashes as his eyes touched her heated cheeks and her mouth and the soft hollow of her throat where a pulse began to beat rapidly. Something about him put her in the strangest panic, revealing a tingling edge of danger.

Meg arrived with the sandwiches, shot a deeply envious look at Lori and departed. 'Eat them!' Brant pushed the plate a little closer to her.

'Aren't you going to have one?' she asked.

'I can make it all right!'

He was looking at her unsmilingly and Lori said a little nervously, 'I don't usually eat at this time of the afternoon.'

'I'd say it was a good idea when you're on the point of collapse.'

She didn't dispute this but began to eat the sandwiches, freshly made for her and delicious with the cold drink. Brant merely watched her, had another drink himself, then when she was finished, came round and held her chair. 'Now I'm going to get you home, but before I do, we'll get a couple of barbecued chickens. I've an idea you might in your desire to please, turn on a roast dinner!'

For some unaccountable reason she was prepared to go along with anything he said. From her state of exhaustion she was now floating on cloud nine. Brant left her in the car when he went in to pick up the chickens and when he came back he was carrying a small cardboard box as well.

'Chocolate cheese cake!' he announced offhandedly. 'I imagine it's delicious for anyone with a sweet tooth. I prefer a cheese board myself, but I know you've got plenty of that!'

'And how on earth am I going to pay you?'

He looked at her pointedly. 'Be pleasant for a change!'

'What a God-awful man!' she exclaimed.

They drove through the golden, somnolent afternoon and Lori was moved to comment on the astonishing display the jacarandas were turning on in the drought. They were blooming everywhere, some of massive size, pushing even the gorgeous poincianas into the shade.

Brant was busy placing a cigarette between his lips and lighting it, but after a minute he said casually, 'They're actually from the high deserts of Brazil. Haven't you ever noticed they go to leaf in the rainy season?'

'So that explains it?'

'It does. They always flower better in the Dry.'

Lori tilted her head back, rayed through with a surprising feeling of wellbeing. Brant's station wagon gave a beautiful ride, and it wasn't steaming hot either as it had been earlier on in the afternoon. Thank heaven she didn't have to ring Di and beg a lift. Involuntarily she sighed and all her tension eased. With the chickens already cooked for her she could toss up a salad and perhaps some tiny new potatoes with a little dressing poured over them while they were hot. She didn't even have to bother with the sweet, and anyway she had a sweet tooth herself. The car was air-conditioned and it was a tonic to feel so beautifully cool...

'Close your eyes!' Brant said quietly.

She resisted for a minute, but her nerves were so soothed her eyelids drooped and she turned her head away from the light. The thin tie straps of her sundress fell off her shoulders, but she didn't even notice, the shirred bodice hugged her tightly and a delicious drowsiness was breaking over her in waves. Sleep was what she needed and it seemed to her it was happening.

CHAPTER THREE

BRANT'S voice and a firm cool hand on her shoulder awoke her. She murmured a little incoherently, still delightfully sleep-drugged, but he shook her.

'Time to wake up, little one!'

She opened her eyes and saw the light framing his head and his shoulders. She was half lying against him, and this fact alone jerked her into wakefulness.

'Oh, I'm sorry!' she said hastily.

'Don't be!' He sounded indulgent, and a half smile hovered about his hard, beautiful mouth.

Lori rubbed a hand over her face and arched her body, throwing up an arm in a graceful unconscious piece of provocation. 'But we're not there yet?' she realised.

'Later on!'

Defying intention, her head slipped back again against the seat. 'I was dreaming!'

'Are you going to tell me?'

'I don't think I can remember.' She turned her head and looked at him and the first flickers of awareness showed in her eyes.

He moved without hurry and drew the soft weight of her body into his arms.

'*No*, Brant!' From languid peace the blood was beating thunderously in her veins.

The dark face above her was vividly, arrogantly male. 'The eternal cry of protest,' he murmured beneath his breath, 'when your eyes tell me something very different!' His fingers threaded through her hair, twisting her head nearer. 'Turn up your mouth, little virgin, because I want it very badly.'

For a dreadful instant Lori thought she was going to cry with the tumultuous shock of it. Sophistication took time and she was so very inexperienced. Her bright, spirited air of independence fell away from her, leaving her trembling, her femininity heightened to a ravishing degree. Urgently she turned her head in a silent plea for understanding, nuzzling the lean bronze column of his neck, but his mouth descended to brush her skin, as sweetly scented and as satiny as a baby's; the eyelids, the curve of her cheek, the corner of her mouth.

It seemed like a ritual torture and she gave an exclamation of frightened pleasure. Brant's hand moved caressingly over the delicate slope of her shoulder and though the shaped bodice of her dress had dipped low to reveal the high, tender swell of her breasts, he made no move to touch her or cup their blossoming sweetness. He just held her captive against him, drugging her senses with what she least expected ... a shuddering, rippling, sensuous gentleness.

'I'm shaking!' she whispered, against his deeply cleft chin.

'I'll stop when you give me your mouth willingly.'

Some vibrant note in his voice was making her very flesh dissolve. She tilted back her head so he could kiss the lovely line of her throat, arching her body with a convulsive little movement. 'I just know in my bones you'll hurt me!' Her own voice sounded strangely haunted and he lifted his head abruptly, staring down at her flushed, flower-like face.

'I expect you've known that for a long time!'

'Sometimes you're kind,' she whispered.

For answer, he clasped her head tightly between his

strong hands and brought down his mouth, kissing her in a way she could never have imagined. Her mouth parted under pressure, fashioned into the shape of his desire. It was so bewildering to have her whole being taken over by this man she had fought for so long. The mingled excitement and shock was almost unbearable, so that even her own will was abandoning her.

Her young agitation betrayed itself in a soft little moan even as an answering storm of passion broke over her. Tears filled her lovely amber eyes and Brant lifted his head imperiously and held her back against his arm.

'Tears, Lori, when I'm trying so hard to treat you gently!'

'I didn't know it could be like this!' she stammered, and his mouth twisted faintly.

. 'I told you you didn't know the first thing about being made love to!'

His arrogant blue-green gaze was striking her face with incomparable assurance, and she stared up at him, the familiar tension back between them.

'And you're going to make it your business to clue me up a little?'

His brilliant eyes narrowed dangerously. 'Be sure of it!'

'Oh, you wicked, calculating beast!'

'So?' he said insolently. 'You were helping me. In fact I was even thinking of abducting you!'

Humiliation raged angrily in her mind. 'Damn you to hell, Brant!'

'Oh, lord!' he sighed wearily, and caught her around the waist. 'Come on, back in your own seat!'

'Don't blame me if your idea went sour on you!'

'Obviously. If you were only a little smarter, you'd be charming!'

She withdrew into a corner, most unnaturally, examining her bare arms for bruises and unexpectedly, his white teeth flashed in a smile.

'If I can be of any more assistance any time, just let me know.'

Fury flashed out of her great amber eyes. 'Don't worry, I'll see you don't commit that particular atrocity again!'

'You weren't in danger for one minute!' he retorted, his glance slanting over her. 'A situation I can't guarantee that will last.'

'And what then?' she taunted him. 'I wouldn't like any gossip to desecrate your good name.'

'How ridiculous!' There was open mockery in his face. 'Come on, put those straps back up on your shoulders and be brave. You've got to grow up some time. Now when Stanton kisses you I only hope you have some basis for comparison!'

'And it didn't mean anything to you at all?'

'Would you have believed me if I said I loved it?' Brant asked wryly, ignoring the pathos in her voice.

'Of course not!'

'Well then, just for the record, I think you're very sweet. Untutored, but sweet.'

'And you know everything you need to know about women!'

'On the contrary. Sometimes I find you absolutely unfathomable. Now you're mad at me!'

The only obvious way to handle him was to ignore him and the sparkling mockery of his gaze. 'Shall we start again for the house?' she asked with forced politeness.

'Of course! I presume your guests will be arriving about seven?'

'Yes,' she said, and was suddenly overwhelmed by her ingratitude. 'Thank you for helping me out.'

'Not as fully as I would have liked!'

'Thank you anyway,' she said briskly so that she wouldn't sound absurd in a situation she couldn't handle.

He reached out a hand and gently stroked back her hair. 'Funny little girl!'

Lori just sat looking in front of her, for the feelings in her heart were so new she didn't even want to own to them. She was a sham, a total sham, and now she knew it she might be able to protect herself. He could, if he wished, drive her mad just by making love to her. Her soft mouth was still tingling from the pressure of his mouth and it was all she could do not to reach up a finger and touch its pulsing cushioned surface. His skin had been as satiny as her own but with a tantalising rasp underneath, and the male scent of him still lingered on her breath and her skin.

So shocked and disturbed was she, she didn't even remember the short trip up to the house. Her whole body was tingling with incredible new sensations and she knew perfectly well she must look a little dazed. Brant pulled into the shade of the sprawling bougain- villea and turned to her with a faint smile in his eyes.

'Everything O.K.?' he asked.

Finally she had to look at him, a flush under her golden skin. 'You had no business kissing me. You only did it to shock me!'

'And obviously I succeeded!' He tilted her chin between his forefinger and thumb. 'You were made for kissing. Just like a baby!'

She swallowed a little and his brilliant eyes softened. 'We'll take it in easy stages!'

That gave her her strength back. 'The devil we will!' she said sharply, and jerked her head away. 'Sometimes I think you like playing cruel games with me!'

'And you definitely don't approve!' His voice was very dry and cool and he got out of the car and went round to open the tail gate.

He was just lifting her parcels out when Dianne came rushing down the stairs, almost powerless to halt herself.

'I've been so anxious about you, Lori. Where have you been?'

'In the pub,' Lori said briskly, and turned to confront her. Anxious, indeed!

Dianne's dark eyes seemed to bore a hole right through the younger girl and Brant said lightly, 'Don't worry, Di. She knows how to behave herself.'

'You're serious, then?' Dianne stared up at him.

'Of course. For some reason Lori found herself left in the lurch. She'll probably tell you the story herself. I merely came to her rescue.'

'Again!' Dianne said, and sighed. 'You're really too good to us. Whose idea was it to sit around drinking?'

'I've forgotten exactly.' He gave Dianne his smooth smile. 'You look very beautiful.'

Dianne started to laugh and looked down at her pretty, low-cut dress. 'This old thing!' She passed the tips of her fingers over the silky skirt. 'Wait until you see what I've got lined up for Saturday night!'

'It should be some occasion!' Brant murmured drily.

Dianne tilted her blonde head to him and smiled. 'When do your guests arrive?'

'They fly in on Friday.'

'Thank heavens they don't have to catch the bus!' Lori said wryly, and Dianne turned to frown at her.

'You look a little intoxicated,' she commented.

'Oh, I am!' she said carefully, then glanced in Brant's direction. 'Thank you again for bringing me home. I'd best go inside and get the preparations for dinner underway.'

'Really, dear,' Dianne said quickly, 'there's very little left for you to do. I've got everything well in hand.'

Lori didn't answer but gave an odd little smile. 'Well, I'll take myself off, anyway. May I have my parcels, Brant?'

'I'll take them up for you,' he said soothingly, and Dianne turned her shining dark eyes on him.

'We're having a small dinner party of our own. I know it's frightfully short notice, but I don't suppose you'd care to join us?'

'Perhaps another time!' He gave her a lazy smile, looking down at her as though the sight of her delighted him. 'I've got a lot of paper work I must get done.'

'Let's name a time!' Dianne countered.

'Why not? How would one night next week suit you? I can't leave Ruth and Jane, of course, but I'd like you both to come up to the house. We can arrange the evening on Saturday. I might ask one or two other people along. Would that suit you?'

'Lovely!' Dianne's long, patrician throat rippled and her eyes glittered in pleasurable triumph as though she had pulled off a coup.

'How about you, kitten?' he included Lori in his indolent smile.

'I'll think about it!' she promised. 'Now I really must *move*!'

'No matter!' Dianne returned sweetly. 'I'll see Brant off. It's grand the way he comes to your aid when you seem bent on making a nuisance of yourself!'

'Which leaves me with nothing to say!' Lori said briefly, and Brant gave his low attractive laugh.

'Naturally I don't find you a nuisance, little one. When a child cries, doesn't one pick it up?'

'Brute!' she said feelingly, and broke away from them. Let them talk their heads off, she didn't care.

As it happened, as she afterwards found out, Dianne had done slightly more than she had been asked to do. The table was beautifully set, the wine glasses polished and an amazingly effective flower arrangement set centre table and just to remind Lori, the antique silver candelabra that were actually quite valuable and Aunt Jocelyn had left to Lori in her will were left out on the kitchen table along with a soft duster and the polish.

Somehow Lori got through the evening, which turned out to be more pleasant than she expected. Dean and Gavin had arrived within minutes of each other and as it was Uncle Viv's weekly crib session at a neighbour's, they had the house to themselves. Lori had more or less expected Dianne to challenge her about the comparative lavishness of the dinner, but apart from a few acid comments about Lori's continually throwing herself upon Brant's good nature she didn't say a word. It was left to Lori to conclude that Dianne didn't know a thing about budgeting, for with the totally unexpected gift of the two mouthwatering barbecued chickens and the superb homemade cheesecake their little dinner party was a great success.

Gavin ate heartily, but he spent most of his time devouring Dianne with his heavy-lidded hazel eyes. Lori didn't altogether like Gavin, there was a thoughtlessness for others in him that she didn't admire, but she had to admit he was attractive with his sun-bleached hair and his smooth brown skin. He wasn't particularly tall, the same height as Dianne in medium heels, which she tactfully was wearing, but his hard body was strong and compact. Perhaps most important to Dianne's way of thinking, the Camfields had money and an excellent grazing property valued at more than a million dollars.

Lori allowed Dianne to take most of the credit for the dinner, and afterwards when Dianne suggested dancing Lori offered to wash up with Dean's help. Dean had been touchingly apologetic all evening and he wasn't one of those males that scorned picking up a dishcloth. Dianne put half a dozen records on the turntable and when the first one began to play she slid her arms around Gavin's rather powerful neck and looked up at him invitingly when he needed no invitation at all. Faintly sighing, Lori finished loading the dinner wagon and wheeled it back into the kitchen where Dean, amazingly, was running all the used dishes under the tap preparatory to washing them in the hot water and detergent. Just looking at him, his beautiful long hands immersed in water and dirty dishes, Lori burst out laughing.

It was what Dean had been waiting for, because Lori had been rather different from her usual self and he couldn't bear to see her anything but happy. 'Just tie an apron around me and I'll wash these,' he offered.

'Not for the first time, I'd say!'

'Mother likes to protect her hands too, but I never use gloves.'

'Good God!' Lori muttered, but came up behind him and tied a frilly cotton apron around his taut waist.

'Love me?' he asked gently, and his blue eyes shone.

'I must admit it's nice of you to help me!' she evaded.

'I suppose Elliot had a few acerbic comments to make about my leaving you.' He turned back abruptly from the sink to stare down into her eyes.

'Not at all!' Lori lied. 'But surely it doesn't make much difference what Brant thinks?'

Dean hesitated, then set a large plate down in the draining tray. 'It does a little. He's one of those people everyone makes a big fuss over. Mother keeps on telling me the wonderful things he's done for the district. The things he's *going* to do. The big plans!'

'Mostly about cotton!' Lori agreed. 'It just could become damned important to this State. Most of it at the moment is grown in New South Wales, but I think Brant plans to change that. We used to have a thriving cotton industry in the old days and Queensland has the most satisfactory climate of all the States, but when prices fell so did the area under cotton—here anyway. Brant means to restore it. He's already floated a private company and he's growing on a large scale even now. Eventually I suppose he might have to give up some of his other interests, although he has a manager on the pineapple plantation!'

'You sound as if you admire him too?'

'But of course!' Lori said in some surprise. 'As a leader of industry. I didn't say as a man...'

'Particularly attractive to women!' Dean pointed

out. 'As I understand it, my dear, he's played around with some extremely fascinating women in his time. It's common knowledge down south where he came from. Mother seems to know a good deal about him and she will insist on telling me. Did you know he was engaged to this cousin of his at one time?'

'*What*?' Lori almost released the fragile wineglass in her shock. 'You mean the one that's coming to stay with him?'

'The very one. Jane Trevelyan she was before her marriage, and according to Mother very like Dianne in type. You know, a long, cool blonde!'

'Well, well!' Lori said faintly. 'I can't imagine any woman getting away from Brant!'

Dean held a dish aloft and stared at her. 'What a curious thing to say. Surely he can lose like everyone else?'

'I wouldn't use that word in connection with him. The one thing he's not is a loser!'

'No need to catch fire!' Dean's blue eyes burned. 'Anyway, I thought I'd prepare you.'

His tone slightly annoyed her and she said rather shortly, 'You haven't broken my heart!'

'Sometimes I doubt if you've got one!'

'Oh, rot!' she said, ignoring the aggrieved, peevish tone. 'Actually I must tell Di. I think she sees herself mistress of a great plantation.'

'Indeed, yes!' Dean returned drily. 'But I doubt if she'll ever make it. Rumour has it he was heartbroken. That's why he came up to Queensland. He's a geologist too, did you know?'

'I am impressed!' Lori managed to speak lightly. 'It's a very complicated story—touching, even. I'd have liked to see Brant with his heart broken. It must have been some time ago. It's mended all the way through!'

Dean let the water out of the sink, dried his hands, took off the apron, then looked round at Lori curiously. 'I'm glad you liked my little anecdote!'

'Well, it gave us something to talk about. I was really pitying that little widow. Brant made her grief seem real enough.'

'Perhaps it was, but life moves on. Someone engineered that visit!'

'Well, no matter anyway!' She stood on tiptoe to put the last wineglass away and Dean came behind her, drawing her back against his heart. 'It was terrible this afternoon, having to leave you.'

'You could have avoided it all by telling me your mother was going. Her dislike of me goes very deep, and I've spent most of my life trying to be polite to her!'

His hands slid up and tried to cup her small breasts, but she broke away from him. 'No, Dean!'

'You're not frigid, are you? How can it always be *no*!' His blue eyes were electric with anger.

'I don't like intimate embraces!'

'Then you *are* frigid!'

'Maybe,' she said quietly, 'but I was brought up to believe a girl should fight all the way for her honour.'

'How terribly sad!'

She stood in the centre of the room looking up at him. 'Have you ever made love to a woman?' she asked.

'Manners, dear. You don't ask those sort of questions. Of course I have, you donkey. It nearly killed me, getting the time away from Mother!'

'Was it good?' Lori asked without thinking, but intensely curious.

He came and stood in front of her, examining her beautifully tinted oval face thoroughly. 'It's still left me with an unresolved passion for you. You'll never, never know your own power. You look like a miracle of desire, yet you won't even let me touch your beautiful breasts. Think how exciting it would be!'

'I'd feel much better if it was the man I was married to!' she said, and flushed delicately.

'And there you are!' His lean fingers clasped her face, pressing lightly on the cheekbones. 'Marry me, Lori. I'll never feel this way about anyone else!'

'And what about your mother?'

'We'll run away!'

'Oh no, we won't!' she said resolutely. 'Your mother would track you down at the ends of the earth. Anyway, you can't run away from your career. I've read all your reviews. The critics think you're terrific and they're waiting for your maturity. So am I!'

He pulled her to him and turned his face into her hair. 'Hell, hell!' he muttered.

'I really care about you, Dean!' she said. 'I want you to succeed.'

Almost beside himself now, Dean put a hand to the back of her head and held her face in position. 'You've got a little-girl mouth—do you know that? Full and tender and silky!' He lowered his head to press his mouth down hard on hers, grinding against her teeth so she had to part her mouth. His little moan of pleasure seemed agonised and she could feel his lean body shivering. Twice in one day she had been kissed and the effect was so different she went limp in his arms, never dazzled or dazed with a white-hot excitement, shocked into a sexual awareness she hadn't the power or will to withstand, but so overcome by physical sympathy she was allowing Dean to do violence to her mouth. She felt no arousal, the embrace wasn't hateful to her; she merely stood helpless, defeated by her own compassionate nature. Dean was her friend, even if his love for her was hopeless. All the rest was lost in an interruption.

The kitchen door swung open and Dianne and Gavin were there, their bright amused gazes flicking over them.

'Charming, just charming!' Gavin drawled, and Dianne laughed delightedly.

'Is this the build-up for an announcement?'

'Could be!' Dean laughed himself, his stretched nerves relaxed. 'What do you say, Lori?'

Her instinct was to protect him from hurt or embarrassment and some of Dianne's tart humour. 'Don't let's commit ourselves at this point!'

'Naturally she's shy!' Dianne said in such a pleased voice Lori scarcely recognised the tone. 'What about coming out now and joining us?'

Gavin was addressing some sotto voce remark to Dean, then finished by clapping him on the shoulder much like a guest at a wedding and Dean expanded visibly, almost playing the perfect groom.

It was too much for Lori. She almost bounded out of the kitchen while Dianne sounded the first four notes of the Wedding March which Gavin took up with a loud:

'Da-da-di-da! Da-da-di-da!'

It was possible, Lori reflected briefly, to be caught up in a situation one didn't want. Sympathy could and did turn into quicksand without warning. It might please Dianne enormously to see her cousin safely married off and out of it, but one couldn't love to order. She had never made Dean any promises, and as he came through the door with his blond hair tumbled and his blue eyes shining right through her, she began to reproach herself for having let him kiss her at all. It was hard to describe her jumbled state of mind, let alone her feelings, but she was certain of one thing! Dean would never suit her as a lover. She didn't want the agonised groping, the little-boy vulnerability. Every nerve in her body demanded the mastery and the discipline she had experienced that afternoon, and it had been only a little part of her schooling.

With his lazy, incomparable skill Brant had turned her into a woman, conscious of her own bewilderingly strong needs. Now, it seemed, when she could have staked anything no woman had ever moved him deeply, his widowed cousin was arriving to share his home and eventually, why not his bed? Even thinking about it made her blush violently, and Dean, mis-interpreting, reached for her with clumsy grace and swept her into his arms.

CHAPTER FOUR

As fate would have it, Lori was the first to meet Mrs Ruth Trevelyan and her daughter Jane. It happened late Friday afternoon when Lori was riding the boundary fence, tense and upset after the morning appointment Uncle Viv had had with Doctor Edmonds. The doctor had come right to the point and confirmed Lori's own anxieties. Uncle Viv needed hospitalisation for his old leg injury and possibly an operation as well as specialised treament for a heart condition neither Uncle Viv nor Lori expected. In fact, at first Uncle Viv had refused to believe it, but sat opposite his old friend and physician, glaring his resentment. Even so, Doctor Edmonds had been adamant and Uncle Viv was to enter hospital as soon as a bed became available, possibly within the week. Dianne, her energies worn down by the continuing heatwave, had declined to go in with them and sit in the surgery, but she too had been very upset at the doctor's diagnosis, angrily suggesting a second opinion.

Uncle Viv had gone to bed to rest and with Dianne storming around the house, bringing up subjects like who was going to pay for it all, and there seemed no need for a private room, Lori found it an intense relief to be out of doors. With the worsening conditions she and Albie were frightened of dingoes coming in to attack the calves, and Albie had ridden out to round up any strays and bring them in for the night.

Lori was just coming down on the creek when she saw, too late, Brant's parked jeep and Brant and two women standing alongside, Brant pointing in the direction of the farm or maybe the billowing smoke haze over Barradon, the highest peak in the range. If she had the power to vanish into thin air Lori would have done it. In her depleted, saddened mood she had no desire to meet anyone, let alone Brant's beautiful, widowed cousin and a mother who from this distance looked scarcely older than the daughter. Both wore classic silk shirts and linen slacks, but while one had gleaming fair hair the other had dark hair pulled back into an elegant updated chignon.

Of course they looked back and saw her and Brant waved a hand, clearly intending her to ride across the creek at the crossing, only a short way along. There wasn't any way she could avoid it, so Lori led her mare along the beaten track and rode across the rippling stones, fixing a pleasant smile on her face.

Brant helped her dismount while the mare stood quietly, then walked to the stream, and Lori found herself facing, if Mrs Stanton's informants were to be believed, the love of Brant's life. She wasn't exactly beautiful, not as beautiful as Dianne anyway, but she had that matchless thing, class. Brant presented her and Lori found both women smiling at her warmly.

'How nice to meet you, Lori, may I?' The older woman spoke first. 'Brant has told us so much about you. You look such a little thing to work so hard!'

Lori took off her hat and her hair blazed in the sun. 'It's funny, but I love it!'

'What gorgeous hair!' Jane exclaimed, apparently sincerely. 'It almost makes me want to change my own colour!'

'Strangely enough Lori doesn't admire her own colouring,' Brant pointed out drily. 'I think she's always hankered after blond hair like her cousin Dianne. You'll be meeting Di tomorrow night.'

'How lovely!' Jane showed her perfect teeth in a smile. 'Brant has just been showing us about the property. It's really marvellous what he's done. 'I've never seen cotton growing before—— All those fluffy white bolls stretching for miles, like white paper daisies in the desert. I'm going to make it my business to find out all about it. After all, cotton is the most important fibre man uses to make clothing!'

'It has other uses too, dear,' her mother pointed out.

'Even cattle feed!' Lori said a little drily. 'The hulls or outer covering of the cotton seed are quite digestible. I expect you'll get to know far more about it than I do. It's not an easy plant to grow but Brant uses all the modern production techniques and we have a very good pilot in the valley to do all the aerial spraying.'

'You run cattle yourself?' Mrs Trevelyan asked kindly. She had very fine grey eyes, the sole feature her daughter had inherited, and they were assessing Lori thoroughly but nicely.

'My uncle does and I help him. This isn't one of our best seasons, but we keep hoping for the rain!'

Jane tilted back her fair head and looked up at the sky. 'No wonder you're worried. One doesn't realise how important the seasons are until one is on the land. It can't be much fun trying to survive a drought.'

'No.' Lori bent her head and looked down at the ground.

'What's wrong, little one?' Brant looked at her closely.

'Just a few worries!' She swung up her head again and smiled at Jane and her mother. 'I guess we all have them.'

'Yes, indeed!' said Mrs Trevelyan, and actually shuddered with recent memories. 'I don't think anyone could say they have no problems at all!'

Lori smiled at her gravely, conscious of the sharp anxiety that had centred round her heart. Uncle Viv was very important to her life. She couldn't imagine it without him, and now with this sudden news about his heart she felt dreadfully afraid.

'If there's anything we can do?' Jane said, after a pause.

'You're very kind!' Lori turned slightly towards her. 'Perhaps I'm being a little over-anxious!'

'Ah!' said Brant. 'It was Viv's appointment this morning, wasn't it?'

'Yes,' she returned briskly so she wouldn't cry.

'Here, dear!' Mrs Trevelyan leaned forward suddenly and patted Lori's arm. 'You tell Brant all about it and we'll walk back to the jeep. It was lovely meeting you, and we look forward to seeing you tomorrow night. You and Dianne.'

Lori looked up and smiled, her great amber eyes shimmering. 'I'm hoping you'll both come across and visit us at the farm. I know Uncle Viv will want to meet you. We're just not certain when he has to go into hospital.'

In spite of the warm, friendly way she spoke both women realised she wasn't far from tears. They said their goodbyes together and strolled off towards the jeep while Lori said a little dully:

'I must go.'

'Just how bad is it?' Brant asked quietly.

'I don't really know. Doctor Edmonds had to speak

very sternly to get Uncle Viv to take any notice of him at all. If the leg fails to respond to treatment, they may have to operate—and that's not the only thing. He has a heart condition, I can't remember the name of it, and I should. It means hardening of the arteries.'

'Arteriosclerosis!' Brant pronounced slowly, and his profile in the golden sunlight looked grim. 'It's a chronic condition, which means he'll always have it, but it can be treated, Lori. Hospital is the best place for him at the moment and he'll be well looked after. What's the delay?'

'There isn't a bed available!' she said and pushed her hat back on her head, adjusting the chinstrap.

Brant looked down at her standing so small and slender at his shoulder. 'How is he taking it?'

'At the moment he's lying down. I don't think he ever suspected about his heart.'

'Perhaps I should come over and see him now,' Brant offered. 'I'll just run Jane and Ruth back to the house.'

'They're very nice,' Lori said briefly, '*and* tactful. I don't know what's the matter with me lately. I've gone all weepy!'

'It will do you good. How's Di reacting?'

'She's upset and worried.'

'And she isn't used to dealing with anxieties.' Brant looked away and frowned slightly. 'Did Doctor Edmonds speak to you both privately or in front of Viv?'

'Well actually, Di didn't go. She doesn't sleep at all soundly in the heat and Uncle Viv didn't want her waiting around in the surgery.'

'It's a good thing it doesn't seem to disturb him about you, otherwise he'd have gone in alone,' Brant commented drily.

His tone had hardened to such an extent it weighed

on her heavily. 'Everyone needs someone to lean on, Brant!'

Feeling incapable of such a thing himself, he stifled his next remark, limiting himself to whistling up the mare. She came obediently, her large dark eyes mildly curious, hoofs and fetlocks wet from the creek. Brant helped Lori mount, then stood there for a moment looking up at her, rubbing an absentminded hand down the mare's glossy neck. 'Don't get yourself into a panic about this. I'll have a word with Doc Edmonds myself. I'm sure with a little extra care Viv will be his old self again!'

'No,' she said simply.

'Stop it, Lori!' he said without violence. 'Give me ten minutes and I'll be over.'

Lori's eyes jerked away from his brilliant aqua gaze. 'I never intended you to come away from your guests.'

'They won't in the least mind!'

'Thank you, Brant...' Her voice trailed away and she lifted her hand to wave at the two slim figures standing by the jeep. They returned the wave and Lori found herself asking when she never even meant to: 'Is it true you were once engaged to Jane?'

'My God!' he said, and shot her a quick look of surprise.

'I'm sorry!' She put her hand to her mouth exactly like a child. 'I can't think what made me say that. It was very impertinent. Anyway, she's lovely!'

'She's that,' he agreed briefly, and his eyes were bright and intent. 'Go on home, Lori, and have an early night. You look worn out.'

He touched the mare's flanks and she responded to the urging picking her way delicately across the creek bed. Lori didn't look back, but she began to feel a little better. Uncle Viv, though taciturn by nature, had always confided in Brant, another man and a man he admired. She was so glad Brant had decided to come across to the farm. Uncle Viv would appreciate the thoughtfulness of the gesture and perhaps he would tell Brant a little more about how he was really feeling.

Eager now to get home, Lori wheeled the mare around at the trees, moving into a canter that quickly lengthened into a gallop. Somewhere at the back of her mind was the thought: Dianne wasn't going to have it all her own way. Brant's young love, Jane, was still a lovely woman with a charm that if turned full on could be radiant. With her beautiful appearance and manner, she was exactly the kind of wife Brant would choose to grace his splendid home. Dianne's chiselled nose when she saw her would be severely out of joint even without the knowledge that once Jane had played an important part in Brant's plans for life. If this was disturbing Lori too, she couldn't allow herself to brood upon it. It simply didn't occur to her that she could seriously interest Brant. He just had an instinct for helping harmless little creatures like herself. Now, feeling exhausted, she was never more grateful for his indomitable strength. She was also frightened. Though it was not to be considered and still incredible to her, she wanted him to catch her up again in the sensual blaze he alone could provoke. Dean had called her frigid, but quite simply she wanted to belong to one man alone. She didn't know it then, but such a hopeless love would soon turn into a devouring anguish.

Brant's visit seemed to ease Uncle Viv's tensions considerably for his look of strain eased almost magically overnight. During the morning Lori finished off the work on her dress and even Dianne reluctantly agreed that it was very pretty and quite professionally made up. Dianne came back from the hairdressers with her blonde hair blown into a sophisticated evening style full of body and movement, but Lori contented herself with a quick shampoo under the shower. With Uncle Viv looking and acting so much brighter she couldn't suppress her excitement. There was always a magic ring to the word *party*, and she hadn't been to all that many of them and none at Brant's house. Gavin, who had dined there many times with his parents, had been very enthusiastic about Brant's life style and Lori still remembered her own awed delight at such luxurious surroundings, and she had only passed very quickly through the front part of the house carrying messages to Brant from Uncle Viv.

By seven-thirty that evening she had her make-up on, secretly rather proud of the job she had done. Though it was absurd to say it, she nearly fell in love with her own likeness—or this new, mysterious likeness, for the foundation covered her skin in a translucent pale gold, shading away the fine dusting of freckles across her nose, and her eyes and her mouth had to belong to somebody else, for they looked extravagantly romantic, her eyes shining like jewels with excitement. This new Lori was impossible to resist, and she smiled at herself in the mirror, her spirits soaring. The synthetic material of her dress glowed with all the colours of the sunset on a gleaming gold ground. It was a brilliant and unusual pattern and on a lot of girls it would have been disastrous, but with Lori's own brilliant colouring it might have been designed for no one else.

She turned away from the mirror, put on her robe and lifted the dress gently off the bed. It just needed the lightest press to be perfect. Uncle Viv was reading the paper at the kitchen table and he gave a little theatrical gasp when he saw her.

'I say, you're a film star, that's it!'

She batted her eyelashes at him and they looked at one another for a long moment in a silence that affected both of them strongly, then Uncle Viv stood up and gathered up his paper. 'I'll finish this in my study and you can get on with your ironing. Come along and show me the final result. Funny, I was just thinking about your aunt and the night we became engaged. She could have had anyone and she chose me. She was a very beautiful girl. Though she was fair, like Dianne, you're much more like her. Silly of me not to have noticed before!'

After he had gone, Lori took up the ironing board from the cupboard and set it up. The iron was already set on synthetic, so she left it standing ready to switch on the power while she arranged the full skirt of her dress over the board. High heels tapped behind her and she turned to see Dianne, fully dressed in her exquisite caftan, outlined against the dark from the other room.

'How do I look?' Dianne demanded confidently.

'Terrific!' Lori murmured sincerely. 'Like the goddess of love!'

For a moment Dianne's long dark eyes glittered, then they narrowed as they swept over Lori's face, seeing her for the first time. 'You've been a bit heavy-handed with the make-up, haven't you?' she commented.

'I can easily correct that!' Lori said quickly. 'You're the expert, tell me where?'

'*Everywhere,* dear!' Dianne returned bluntly. 'If we had time I'd advise you to wash it all off and start

again. As it is you'll have to do something to tone
down your eyes and your mouth. You look too brilliant, darling, if you know what I mean!'

'Actually I went very sparingly. I guess it's my
colouring.'

Dianne laughed gently as she would at a school-
girl's first efforts. 'And that of course is the problem.
You've got too much colour in your hair!'

'So you've been telling me for years. Anyway, no
one will be taking much notice of me.'

Dianne lifted her hand and touched it to her long
throat. 'Well, you didn't think you were going to
compete with *me*, for heaven's sake?'

'I've never thought that. Actually I was talking
about Jane.'

From languor and an arching throat Dianne's tall
body went tense. 'What about her?'

'Didn't I mention it?' Lori lifted her head wryly.
'She's perfectly beautiful. Not in your way, but in her
own way.'

Dianne's voice had the quick flip of a whiplash.
'But she's well into her thirties, so I've heard.'

Lori shook her head. 'That has little to do with it.
I'm merely stating a fact. She's a very lovely woman.
You might as well be prepared. The truth is, I'm
afraid, Brant was engaged to her at one time.'

'You're lying!' Dianne's scarlet mouth thinned
with anger.

'I don't think so. At least Mrs Stanton claims it's
true, and she's not the kind of woman to spread gossip
or make mistakes. I was as surprised as you!'

Dianne faced her unsmilingly from the door.
'You're getting a kick out of this, aren't you?'

Lori's fingers lifted to the power switch as she
turned on the iron. 'I'm sorry I told you. I didn't

mean anything except to prepare you.'

Dianne made a sound of infinite contempt. 'I'm not such a fool I'll believe that. You've always been jealous of me, haven't you?'

'*No!*' Lori shook her head. 'Jealousy is not my way. It's you, Dianne, who have never been *my* friend.'

'Try and remember, cousin, there's always a reason. It doesn't matter to me that Brant's old flame is good-looking. She's nearly ten years older than I am and that gives me an enormous advantage. Just one little thing, don't *you* get any ideas about Brant.'

'And what could you do about it if I did?' Lori returned with spirit.

'Try it and find out!' Dianne's eyes had turned almost black and Lori swept past her. 'If I don't hurry we'll be late!'

Trembling for a moment in her bedroom, Lori told herself she had to go back into the kitchen and collect her dress, but at least by moving she had broken up a bad moment. Dianne was very unpredictable and she had to believe herself the most beautiful and desirable woman for miles around, almost like the wicked queen in Snow White. After the short breathing space she went back into the kitchen and found Dianne had gone. She went quickly to the ironing board, picked up the iron and brushed it lightly over the gleaming material.

It shrivelled up almost immediately, crinkling her nostrils with the acrid smell, leaving a great gaping hole. Her distress was so acute she didn't even cry out. How could she have been so foolish as to put tempta-tion in Dianne's way? Every little mean act of their girlhood came back to her. The hundred and one little ways Dianne had found to make her young cousin suffer. A sense of utter futility came upon her. She couldn't make a scene and upset Uncle Viv. She couldn't overwhelm them both with the truth of Dianne's malice. There was only one thing she could do: stay home.

Lori took her ruined dress from the ironing board, put everything neatly away, careful to turn the setting on the iron away from cotton/linen back to synthetics, then, that done, she went along the passageway quietly to Dianne's room and pushed open the door.

'Do you feel any pride in what you've done?'

Dianne moved casually away from the triple mirror on her dressing table. 'What on earth are you talking about?'

'This!' Lori held up the scarred dress. 'Just one of the hundred of your small catty ways!'

Dianne's delicate brows lifted almost to her hair line. 'Are you mad?' she drawled.

'Oh, I think not!' Lori returned gravely.

'And what are you going to do? Go to Dad with your wild concocted story? I'll only deny it. Obviously you left the iron on the wrong setting.'

'It hardly matters now,' Lori said with a shrug. 'Go to the party, Dianne, and good luck to you. This is between the three of us—you and me and your conscience!'

For the first time Dianne showed a chink in her armour and a flush mounted her cheekbones. Nevertheless she spoke in her usual arrogant manner. 'Oh, don't be so melodramatic! Surely you can wear something else?'

Lori shook her head. 'I'm afraid my interest in the evening has vanished. You can make my excuses for me. I'll borrow one of Mrs Stanton's migraines.'

Dianne made a little jeering sound. 'Anyone would think the loss of one dress was a disaster! Dean is counting on you to be there. It seems to me you could show more ingenuity and pull out something else.'

Lori considered this for a moment with wry humour. 'You know darned well I haven't got anything else. That material was very expensive—and listen here, you're going to pay for it!'

'You're joking!' Dianne's face was one of hard confidence. 'Maybe it's best if you do stay home after all. You're not quite right in the head, are you? Coming in here and accusing me of ruining your dress. As if I would!'

'Forgive me if I'm not impressed with your display of innocence. It's the greatest source of surprise to me you're your mother's daughter!'

Dianne looked up quickly and her burning rage showed in her face. She took a few quick steps forward and slapped Lori hard across the face. 'Don't you talk to me about my mother! You did your best to steal her love from me!'

'Think again, cousin!' Lori said sombrely. 'I didn't have to do a thing. Could anyone have more insight into a soul than a mother?' She turned away with a youthful, eloquent dignity, her revulsion shining out of her eyes. 'Enjoy yourself while you can. Life has a way of paying us out in our own coin!'

Dianne tried to summon up something withering, but she couldn't quite make it. She turned about quickly to see if anything of the ugly episode was showing in her flawless appearance, but she didn't think so. She collected her evening purse, checked to see if it contained everything she wanted, then she went out into the hallway and along the passageway to her father's study. She knew just how to put it, expressing her concern and dismay, and presently Lori would come along and verify her story. Poor little bleeding heart Lori!

Bit by bit Lori regained her tranquillity, so that by the time an hour had passed she was almost calm and resigned. Uncle Viv had been sorely dismayed at the accident to her dress, but didn't try to persuade her to go to the party against her own inclination. Feeling appropriately dressed was important to a woman, he realised that, and it was the greatest pity Lori couldn't take advantage of Dianne's magnanimous offer to 'borrow anything at all' from her wardrobe. Lori was petite and Dianne was tall, with a wide-shouldered, long-waisted figure that severely limited Lori's borrowing power. The offer was absurd, of course. Lori knew perfectly well it wasn't meant, but in spite of the blow she had been dealt she wasn't going to betray her cousin to the father who loved her and endowed her with qualities she simply didn't possess.

Shortly before nine, Uncle Viv went off to bed and Lori found herself getting out the materials she had in mind for a huge, triple-tiered hanging plant holder. Her smaller versions had been very successful and it was time now to turn to a more ambitious work. It was merely a matter of getting through the evening, and she could hardly put her head down and cry. It was only a short time ago anyway that her numbed mind had come round to considering an alternative outfit; not that anything she possessed could replace the ruined dress, but she was normally nothing if not resourceful. She couldn't have looked unforgettable and madly expensive like Dianne, but she could have worn her little crocheted top with the ruffled skirt she had made. She looked her best in simple things anyway, forgetting she had the priceless advantage of a small, perfect body. Dianne's revenge had been complete, for she had even numbed Lori's mind.

The sound of a car approaching had her springing to her feet. She threw down her work and hurried out on to the veranda. The dogs were out so they would set up their barking and disturb Uncle Viv, so Lori whistled them up softly and they came racing out of the shadows and up on to the veranda to stand each side of her while she held their collars.

The big station wagon came to a halt at the very base of the stairs and Brant swung out, so impeccably groomed and so formidably handsome, she tossed her head in an effort to clear it. The dogs were straining to go down and welcome him, but he called a firm order to them and they sat back on their haunches obediently, realising that for once he wasn't in the mood to encourage their usual display of affection.

Lori continued to stand wide-eyed, feeling in some way she had to placate him, for his tall frame gave off a considerable emanation of suppressed anger. His sand-coloured linen suit showed off to perfection his dark tan and his open-necked blue shirt had the sheen of silk—but she only had time to admire those things later, for his eyes were blazing like a flash of summer lightning and she realised she had to defend herself for staying away from his party.

'Well?' His single question confirmed her notion.

'Well what?' she parried laconically.

For answer he dismissed the dogs and pulled her inside the house. 'Dianne told me you begged off at the last minute with a bad head, but you look perfectly all right to me—in fact I've never seen you looking better!'

'Honestly... it passed off!'

'Stop it!' he said tersely. 'I hate lies!'

A few other things she noticed. The glinting gold medallion round his neck, the curl of fine black hair, the overpowering masculinity that made her breathing urgent and deep. 'Why bother about me?' she said with biting humour. 'Haven't you got enough women falling over you?'

For a minute Brant looked as if he meant to slap her, and she even turned her head, tense and wary. Even the lightest blow from Brant would put her on the ground, but it was soon apparent that he was exercising a considerable degree of control. 'What an ignorant little girl you are!' he murmured, and his voice had a fine, goading edge. 'It's apparent you don't consider my feelings for one moment, or the feelings of my guests. Ruth and Jane were looking forward to seeing more of you, let alone your quite lunatic friend Stanton. He went into a marked decline with Di's news. Pretty soon he won't be able to take a breath without you!'

'I'm sorry,' she said, and her eyes ranged over his face with anxiety for Dean, 'but his mother's there, isn't she?'

'My darling child,' he said grimly, 'it's perfectly well known to me, if not you, that Stanton is prepared to jettison his mother if he can have you. I'm even wondering if he'll ever play the piano again without you. Certainly not tonight without your support!'

'He'll manage!' Lori returned crisply. 'He'll have to!' She was standing under the light and her hair was a glory, each silky strand glinting fire, metallic in its appearance but baby-soft to the touch.

'But wouldn't you like to please him? I know you don't give a damn about me. I just come in handy at the odd time!'

She swung around to face him, catching the jewelled flash of his eyes. 'You're really angry, aren't you?'

A muscle jerked beside his mouth and he didn't even hesitate. 'I confess to being slightly annoyed with you. I told myself you were improving, but you're still the same thoughtless little girl!'

'It's not true!' said Lori a little wildly, infected by his manner.

'Then why concoct a stupid headache?'

'Because ... because. ...'

'Why?' he asked curiously, seeing something different about her, the unbearable distress she had carefully bottled up.

For answer she walked away across the room and came back with her glowing, ruined dress in her hand. 'A girl needs the right dress for the right occasion. Unfortunately I had an accident with the iron, and I've never liked the smell of burning!'

Brant took the dress from her and held it up closer, examining the scorched area. 'How the devil did you do that? It's synthetic, isn't it?'

She nodded her head. 'I could have made even *you* take notice in that!'

He glanced up quickly and something in his changing expression made excitement spurt through her every vein. 'Right at this minute I can't understand how this happened, but now it's not even important. We have to get back to the party. Go and put on something else!'

'I won't look the same!' she warned him.

'You'll look good no matter what!' he said drily. 'Poor little Lori, what was it intended as, a form of punishment?'

'I'm not with you,' she said on a sharp intake of breath. 'I told you it was an accident.'

'Was it? Ten minutes ago I could have strangled

you with my bare hands, now I'm prepared to indulge your every fantasy. Go away and change, we're wasting time!'

Colour rushed up under her skin as she was swept with a brilliant excitement. 'Won't they be missing you?'

'Yes.' There was a disturbing hint of self-mockery in his voice. 'Is Viv asleep?'

'Yes.'

'Then go quietly. I'll give you fifteen minutes!'

'I'll take less!' She made a lightning dancing move out of the room, feeling so much like Cinderella it made her afraid to be so happy.

CHAPTER FIVE

AFTER the comfortable unpretentiousness of the farm, Brant's place seemed like Paradise, so that Lori had to adopt a certain cool in case she stood about with her mouth open. The large white colonial-style residence, though single-storey, had grown and grown over the years into a house of impressive size and it was decorated with innumerable paintings and antiques as well as particularly luxurious modern pieces of seating.

A flight of four steps led up to the covered veranda so necessary in the tropics, the succession of French doors flanked by louvred shutters painted a dark green. Outside lights were concealed in the abundant lush foliage and great saucer-shaped planters stood at intervals along the wall, heavy with blossoming shrubs and all manner of philodendrons and orchids in rich, massed planting. Orchids too were suspended from the sloping roof, the hanging dendrobiums, the beautiful showy 'Cooktown Orchid', the State flower, in deepest cerise, and there were great cascades of hybrids in varying shades.

Brant stopped by the golden dendrobium and broke off a cluster of three flowers from the hanging bracts.

'Put this on your shoulder or in your hair,' he ordered. 'God knows you look exotic enough!'

'I hope that's a compliment?' said Lori, a little uneasily, for she wasn't really happy about appearing in a clingy little bodice and a colourful skirt.

He passed her the orchids, his aquamarine gaze

flicking over her. 'You couldn't look better if you'd
planned it for ever!'

'Why, thank you!' she said demurely, and smiled
into his eyes. 'Maybe Jane will lend me a clip and I'll
put them in my hair. Cream and gold—I love those
colours!'

'They belong to you.'

There was no uncertainty about her now and she
preceded him into the spacious central hallway. A
great sunburst of hand-cut crystal hung above her
head, every piece as flawless as a diamond, nearly
blinding her for a moment. There was the sound of
music and laughter, then Jane was coming out towards
them from the direction of the living room, exceedingly elegant in a chiffon dress the changing colour of
the sea, a blue-green like Brant's eyes.

'Oh, how lovely! You're back!' She came gliding
forward as graceful as a swan and took Lori's hand.
'I'm so glad you could make it!'

'Thank you, Jane.' Lori held the outstretched hand
as cool and fragrant as a lily. 'You look beautiful!'

'So do you. Now what are you going to do about
those orchids?'

'I'm sure you can lend Lori a pin or a clip or some
such thing,' Brant said lightly.

'Of course I can!' Jane ran experienced eyes over
Lori's slender form. 'I think your hair. Just a little
behind the ear. Come with me to my room. We'll find
something.' She turned back to Brant for a moment.
'By the way, darling, Senator Marsh has arrived.'

'Good!' Brant returned briefly. 'We might be able
to mix a little business with pleasure!'

'I can't promise you that!' Jane smiled engagingly.
'He's already started on the whisky!'

Brant struck his hand to his temple and took off

with a flourish while Jane led Lori away laughingly. Lori's dazzled and inherently artistic eye couldn't find fault with anything. She went to compliment Jane most sincerely on the exquisite floral arrangements in the Japanese style, but Jane was forced to disclaim them. Brant's manservant Shillito had been responsible for those and they were stunning in their superb austerity, making much use of unusual leaves and Oriental porcelain containers and fragrant white flowers, gardenias and angel orchids and the unbelievably beautiful giant 'Belle de Nuit', fully nine inches across the iridescent white waxy petals.

With Jane so pleasant and friendly, it was easy to relax, and Lori was never more sure Jane would make the perfect mistress for such a beautiful home. Her ease and familiarity with Brant was plain to see, and Lori had many opportunities to witness their poised and relaxed understanding in the hours ahead. Jane was never very far from his side, a most charming hostess, her intelligent, very expressive face aglow.

'They make the perfect couple, don't they?' Dean observed in her ear. 'They'll probably make an announcement tonight!'

Lori glanced backwards and Dean slipped into the chair beside her. He was carrying two glasses of champagne and he passed one to her. 'I'm sure you can allow yourself one!'

'I'm not used to it,' she protested, her heavy lashes veiling her look of piercing shock. Much as she liked Jane she couldn't bear the thought of her married to Brant. Brant was so marvellously free, so fascinating, whether he was hard and withdrawn or lazily indulgent, and if he was married he would be neither of those things to her anymore. She couldn't bear it, and she didn't dare to elaborate any more on her feelings.

The champagne made her feel slightly giddy and as Dean was waiting to play his party piece he didn't have another glass either. 'What's wrong, sweetie, you've gone very quiet?'

'I was just wondering how they ever parted in the first place,' confessed Lori.

'What does it matter?' Dean returned. 'They're pretty absorbed in one another at the moment—and isn't darling Di's nose out of joint?'

Through the open sliding glass wall they could see Dianne sitting at the poolside with Gavin. Quite a few were swimming, but Dianne had her long graceful limbs arranged on a redwood lounger, plushly upholstered. Her gauzy silver caftan glittered little stars and she seemed to be giving more attention to Brant's laughing group inside than ever she was giving the adoring Gavin.

'Poor Di!' Lori murmured, always reluctant to go on condemning her cousin.

'Why doesn't she settle for Gavin?' Dean half whispered. 'She must know twenty-five is almost over the hill for a model.'

'Don't say that!' Lori said quickly.

'It's true. She's a beautiful girl, I admit, but the camera soon shows up every horrifying little wrinkle!'

He sounded so bitchy Lori frowned. 'You've never liked Di, have you?' she said.

'To her great surprise, no. Don't be mad at me, darling, I know you're a loyal little thing, but Di is selfish to the bone. Look how long she's kept away from her father. I'll bet it hurt him. She must have been well paid, yet she didn't come back with a bag full of presents or even offers to help out. And *don't* tell me she didn't have something to do with ruining your dress. I know Di—or women like Di. Threaten them and they turn into tigresses!'

'She's not happy, all the same,' Lori said quietly.

'And why should she be? She doesn't deserve it. Anyway, quite apart from the shock of ruining your dress that little outfit is quite fetching. Your figure is ideal for those clingy little tops. You're really a pocket Venus—and I just love the orchids. Where did you get them?'

'That was Brant's idea,' she said, a little distracted by Jane's merry peal of laughter.

'Oh, really?' Deliberately Dean turned her chin back to him. 'It might be better if you give your full attention here. Brant Elliot is much too experienced and sophisticated for demure little girls like you. Besides, it would amount to cradle-snatching!'

Lori was saved having to answer, for Jane broke away from her admiring circle of friends to come towards them, fixing her sparkling grey eyes on Dean's face.

'I hope you're going to be true to your promise, Dean?' she asked charmingly. 'I'd love to hear you play, and I'm sure that goes for all of us. Would you mind?'

Dean was already standing and he gave a slight, rather elegant bow. 'I'd be delighted to.' He turned his gleaming blond head and looked down at Lori. 'Come and sit beside me.'

'Not on the piano stool, surely?'

He merely grasped her hand and drew her to her feet. 'Let's see.'

The grand piano was full size, a magnificent Steinway backed dramatically by a gorgeous Oriental screen, all flowers and birds mixed together. Cym-

bidium orchids in a gleaming green and bronze flow-
ered profusely out of a large cloisonné pot that Shillito
had placed on the closed lid, and Jane gestured towards it as if asking Dean did he want it removed.

Undoubtedly with the parquet floor scattered here
and there with Kelim rugs he would get considerable
resonance from the piano even with the lid closed, and
his mood seemed to be definitely lighthearted. In front
of them and his mother's anguished eyes he spanned
Lori's narrow waist with his strong hands and lifted
her in a single fluid movement to sit on the piano, her
slender legs curving into the bend.

Happily she kept her head and even smiled, looking
more entrancing than she ever knew in such a beautiful, exotic setting, a flowering bract of the orchids
caressing her bare arm and curving over her shoulder.
Others beside Dean must have decided she looked
very well there, because a delighted burst of applause
and some laughter broke out.

Involuntarily Lori's gaze flew across the room to
Brant as though appealing to him to rescue her, but he
merely raised one eyebrow and left her sitting there
feeling tremulous. There was a curious glint in his blue-
green eyes, but his dark face was smooth and enig-
matic. Brant was a riddle, and she could never figure
him out. Dean was saying something to Jane and she
gave a soft little laugh, then turned away with the
promise to quiet everyone out on the terrace.

They heard her calm voice, then a minute later she
came back into the room and sank with a lovely swirl
of her skirt on to the sofa beside Brant. Dean was
already seated at the piano looking up at Lori, then as
a hush took hold of them all he brought down his
right hand on a brilliant trill that led him into the fiery
and highly rhythmical Ritual Fire Dance, one of his

set 'party pieces' and instantly recognisable to almost everyone.

From the instant his hands touched the keyboard it seemed to Lori that Dean changed into a different person. His look of sensitive vulnerability hardened into authority and concentration firmed up the mouth and jawline. This was his own world and the only one he seemed properly able to function in. She forgot her own shyness and the slight feeling of looking ridiculous poised up on the piano, and let the powerful beat of the music take charge of her.

When he had finished there was no need for anyone to force themselves to applaud. The performance had been brilliant by any standards and there were several urgent calls for encores, including Mrs Trevelyan's request for a Chopin polonaise. It was the moment Lori decided to slip down from the piano, and Brant, with his eyes trained on her expressive face, reached her side and lifted her down smoothly, keeping his hand on her shoulder.

'That was superb, Dean!' he gave the younger man the accolade. 'I think we'll have the lid up this time and give the piano the opportunity to really sound. It's unlikely we'll ever hear it played so well again!'

As Brant was speaking, Shillito on hand, removed the orchids from the lid of the piano and set them down on a side table, then he moved unobtrusively to lift the lid. Brant nodded to him and he bowed without expression and removed himself to the far side of the room to listen, a slight, ascetic figure immaculately uniformed.

As Lori came away from the piano with Brant, Mrs Stanton lost her frozen expression. She had suffered the sight of Lori's vivid presence long enough; now she could enjoy her son's playing with her whole person and not continually fight the impulse to slap Lori to her knees. After all, it was she from whom Dean had inherited his gift and she again who had devoted her life to developing his great talent. As she passed Mrs Stanton Lori received all these impressions and the Senator found her a place beside him with a quick, over-bright smile. At least Brant was safely close by, shifting slightly so he could observe her delicate profile.

Dean's playing was to impress itself upon everybody. In deference to Mrs Trevelyan he played the Chopin polonaise at once, then concluded with a Liszt Rhapsody that showed his stunning technical virtuosity to advantage. Elated and relaxed at one and the same time, he stood up from the piano amid the familiar applause he was used to and his blue eyes were already seeking Lori out as though it was essential he restore her to his side.

'Aren't you glad you came?' Brant asked drily near her ear.

She answered with an odd little smile, her nerves tightened by the music. She might be nothing more than a nuisance to Brant, but lately her own feelings towards him had become cruelly illuminated. The fact that he had kissed her had become a crisis in her young life and it left her yearning blindly for more. Some expression in his eyes was arresting her, keeping her locked in a palpable silence. If he only knew how violently her heart was beating—and she could see no sense or end to it all.

'Are you listening?' he asked.

'Yes, I am.'

'Come and dance with me.' He smiled across her at the Senator, who turned back that minute too late. 'Excuse us, won't you, Roland?'

'I'll have to,' the Senator said lightly. 'I feel quite disappointed you beat me to it. Never mind, Jane and I will make a job of it!'

Outside on the terrace Lori shivered as she encountered Dianne's rigid gaze. She didn't have to search her mind either to realise that Dianne was madly jealous and Lori would be on the receiving end of some pretty intolerable comments. Dianne had never expected to see her here this evening, much less caught into Brant's strong arms.

'What's the matter now?' he asked.

'Why, nothing!' She lifted her bright head a little defiantly. 'How could anything be wrong at a wonderful party like this? Your house is beautiful and Shillito is a treasure. I've never seen such exquisite floral arrangements!'

'He'll gladly show you if you ask him. Shillito used to manage my mother's household, but when she died he came to me. He's a very cultured and cultivated man and incredibly soothing to have around. The house runs as smooth as clockwork, and all due to Shillito.'

'What happens when you take a wife?' she asked him. 'Surely you'll have to sooner or later?'

'I expect so,' he said coolly.

'Do I detect an aversion to my question?' She gave him a veiled glance, aware of his extraordinary attraction, the dark bronze of his skin accentuated by the pale cloth of his jacket, the blue-green flick of his eyes. 'Jane is lovely,' she said.

'Are you trying to persuade me to marry Jane, by any chance?'

'She's exactly the kind of woman I'd expect you to marry,' she returned swiftly.

'Then why are you trying to get me to make love to

you?' he asked her bluntly, and in the curve of his mouth there was a suggestion of subtle cruelty.

The shocking truth of it made her wince. 'Let me go!' she muttered.

'Oh no, you're not going to get away so easily!' The arm about her waist tightened, setting up a faint, quivering pain.

Lori leaned back against it and gave him a surprised glance. 'I think you get some small pleasure out of hurting me!'

'So you've said before. Actually I like to shake you up a little—and you know why. For your own good. Right this minute Stanton's standing by the door wondering numbly how he's going to cut in. I hope you realise now how deeply he's in love with you, and he mightn't be reasonable about it if you can't feel the same way. You've only got to look at him to see how he'd take to frustration.'

'I suppose you think I've been a fool to let it happen?' She searched his dark face.

'Well, little one, I don't think these things actually enter your head. I have to keep reminding myself you're the complete little innocent.'

'I am *not*!' she protested, breathless at his touch.

'Tell me about it.' He looked down at her with mocking disbelief.

'Well, of course, you don't answer me, so why should I answer you? *Were* you engaged to Jane?' she burst out in a different voice.

He looked down at her reprovingly. 'Her husband wouldn't stand for it!'

'All right!' she said shortly. 'It doesn't matter.'

'But it seems to, Lori. Who told you that, by the way?'

She wanted to shout: Mrs Stanton! but she didn't.

'Are you afraid to say it?'

She glanced up at him, painfully aware of the force of her passions. 'Naturally I can't reveal a confidence.'

'It doesn't matter—I've a fair idea. What does surprise me is that *you* should tackle me about it. I mean, you've obviously looked on me as that brute across the creek.'

'Generally you act like it,' she said huskily.

'At least I fetched you tonight,' he reminded her. 'I didn't want to see Stanton's evening ruined.'

'You're very considerate all of a sudden!' She tilted her head and fixed her shimmering eyes on him. Excitement was heightening the colour in her skin, and the light seemed caught in the gleaming, glinting cloud of hair. There was undeniably a tension between them, but she couldn't break away from him, for his arm had tightened to steel. She didn't know it, but she looked very beautiful and intense, unable in her youth and inexperience to hide her only half-conscious wild longings.

Searching her oval face, his eyes darkened to pure green and his male arrogance shrivelled her like a flame. Though she despised herself for doing absolutely nothing about it, when Brant stopped and asked her casually if she would like to see over the rest of the house, she gave a vague little gesture he interpreted as yes.

He took her elbow, nodded pleasantly in Dean's anxious direction and steered her along the terrace that ran the full length of the house and looked out on the pool and informal entertainment area. The scent of gardenias was heavy in the air, blossoming hectically all around them, not even giving Lori a chance to think clearly. Several rooms along Brant pulled open the sliding glass door and drew her inside, shutting the door after him. The sounds of laughter and splashing from the pool were immediately muted, but Lori felt utterly defenceless until he turned on the light. She was really in a highly nervous state altogether and he laughed softly with an ironic kind of tenderness and reached out to flick on the light.

'Poor Lori! You came with me. You know you did!'

'Won't you show me what you were going to?' She looked vaguely round the room that she now saw was the library. Bookshelves lined the walls and paintings hung here and there. The furnishings were heavily masculine. There was a large desk to one side of the room and several deep, comfortable armchairs. 'Is this your den?'

'No, but it's somewhere I often escape to. Do you want to look at some first editions or do you prefer talking?'

'I don't feel like either!' She closed her eyes, looking positively tragic, and Brant reached for her with gentle violence and drew her into his arms.

'Perhaps it will turn out that we have something in common after all?'

Lori shook her head but wouldn't lift it, and he gave her hair a slight tug. 'There, that's better! I've never seen a girl with golden fire in her eyes.'

'If I had any sense at all I'd run away,' she whispered.

'Instead of which you're deliberately leading me up the garden path.'

His expression was mocking as though he was fond of strange amusements, and Lori's temper flared. 'Oh, I hope one day you get your just deserts!'

'Perhaps I will.' His brilliant eyes were heavily shadowed by his lashes. 'Why don't you help me?'

'*I* won't!' she said in a clipped little voice, and pushed against him like a tortured child.

It was no use. His arm slid along her back, holding her close to him. 'This has been a memorable night altogether and I see no reason why it should end here!'

For all her pounding blood she made a futile bid at self-protection. She brought up her hand and held it against her mouth, but he effectively pushed it aside and pinned her wrist.

'No more games, Lori!' he said almost curtly. 'You're more flagrantly a woman than anyone I know!'

His face was all hard planes and shadows and there was a brilliant urgency in his eyes.

Tomorrow would be very unpleasant, but tonight would be sweet. All thought of resistance vanished from Lori's mind. She moved against him, the tilt of her breasts against his taut chest, her head falling back, the light glinting in her hair, her lips parting as though she could feel his mouth against her own. A dangerous tide of feeling was racing between them and he gave a muffled exclamation and lowered his head abruptly, pressing his mouth down hard on hers as though she was an object of his frustrated passion.

For an instant he hurt her, but she gave herself up to him, almost drowning in sensation, and the intimation of the ecstasy she could never share with him. Her soft mouth quivered under that strangely urgent assault, then she became aware that his hard touch had eased to swathe her in total security and an effortless passion.

'I love you!' she whispered, and sighed deeply in resignation, but Brant never even heard her, almost moodily covering her face in kisses, then coming back to her mouth as though he would seek out her very soul.

Lori couldn't begin to explain herself. She wasn't even the person she thought she was, but everything about him was challenging her to prove herself a woman for a single night. He was to blame for her downfall anyway. He alone knew how to rouse her. When he lifted her off the ground, she locked her small golden hands behind his head, knowing full well she could be anything he wanted if only he let her. It was a curiously dreamlike experience to be held in his arms, languorous and drowsy yet wondrously alive. One hand came down and touched his cheek, savouring the feel of it, one fingertip fitting into the deep cleft in his chin. The skin of his throat was very brown and firm, and powerless now to stop herself, she let her hand slip inside the collar of his shirt, stroking the sensitive fingertips over the hard bone of his shoulder. It was electrifying to be able to touch him. He had been so remote from her like some superior being from another planet, but there could be no doubt of the heavy human beating of the heart beneath her hand. She wanted him badly in a way she had never dreamed of, every bone in her body melting away so she lay fluid against him, bound to him by her upraised arms.

It took her fully a minute to realise they were only passing through one room to another. He had no intention of making love to her. He had her in his grasp and he didn't want her. Oh, what a fool she was! A poor, foolish, lost girl. Would she ever recover her pride? Until he had kissed her she didn't know how very much he meant to her; now he was enjoying keeping her in the position of suppliant. That was what it was all about, of course. He loved power. It was the way his mind worked.

When he set her down, she had to lean against the wall for support. His hand in her hair had loosened the spray of orchids and now they fell forward down her cheek and on to the crimson Turkey rug. This room was smaller, a sitting room or an adjunct of the library, she wasn't certain. A writhing humiliation was producing in her a host of new feelings and a seething love-hate. She, so proud and stubborn, had told Brant she loved him. It didn't seem possible she could have uttered the words, but his kisses and the caressing touch of his hands had acted like some dreadful truth drug calling up her subconscious. Now at this moment she wanted to run and hide from him and never know what love was. It was true what he had once said of her; she had no understanding of men.

Brant picked up the golden orchids and set them to one side, then looked down at her, her head half averted from his gaze. 'Why look like that, Lori?'

The question was unexpectedly gentle and she trembled. 'I'm sorry, I don't know how I look!'

'Then I'll tell you. A little while ago you told me you loved me, now you look like a frightened little lamb left alone with a tiger. No harm was done to you, was it?'

'I can't even talk about it!' she said beneath her breath.

'Obviously not!' His white teeth seemed to snap. 'You're a perverse little creature, an enchantress one moment and the outraged little innocent the next. I take no pleasure out of hurting you, as you seem to think!'

'That's funny, I don't believe you!' she said hotly.

There was no tenderness in his dark face or the curve of that beautiful hard mouth. He was so terrifyingly sure of himself he made her feel painfully inhibited, apparently a little puritan. She could have wept for her own betrayal, telling him she loved him. All she could do now was deny it.

'The important thing,' he said curtly, 'is that you know exactly how to respond. In my arms you'll deny me nothing, but the minute I let you go you rush right out of my grasp like some frightened little idiot!'

'But I am!' she cried brokenly, 'and you can make all the fun of me you like. It might be completely natural to you to make love to any woman you like, but I've never had a lover in my life!'

For a few seconds he stared at her, like some rare butterfly under glass, then hatefully he laughed, and the humour of it was reflected in his brilliant eyes. 'Right now you couldn't handle one!'

Lori hit out at him in a frenzy and he endured her small fists, then he pinned her wrists behind her and jerked her towards him. 'Say you love me again!'

'*Never*! I only wanted to see how you'd react anyway. Brant Elliot, the supreme egotist!'

'I'm not, little one. But one day I'm going to make love to you for hours on end. It's the only thing I can think of to cure you!'

She gave a helpless little sigh, still enormously excited but determined to destroy his power over her. 'Please let me go!' she whispered.

'Certainly!' His hands dropped away from her, and despite herself she swayed. 'I'm convinced I won't be able to have an intelligent conversation with you for at least another five years!'

'Just promise me you'll start tomorrow. *Not* speaking to me, I mean!'

'You horrid little girl!'

'That's fine!' she said shortly. 'I don't like you either!'

'No, but you love me.'

His eyes were so brilliant and mocking she couldn't bear them on her. 'Surely you don't believe every word a woman says to you. I just went temporarily out of my mind. I'll bet it's happened to lots of girls you've kissed!'

'Maybe,' he said drily, 'but you're the first child I've ever tried to make love to—though it didn't occur to me at the time!' His gaze narrowed over her flushed cheeks and sparkling eyes and became frankly cynical. 'All right, little Saint Lorinda, I can see you struggling valiantly with your temper, let's go back to the others!'

'I'm ready!' she flashed at him, the whole atmosphere explosive. 'Oh wait, my orchids!'

'Good God!' he said in grim surprise. 'Don't tell me you want them!'

'Why not?' she caught them up with trembling fingers. 'They're beautiful. It doesn't really matter that you gave them to me!'

'What frightful manners!' his laugh was brief and harshly amused. 'I'm really worried about you, Lori!'

'No need to be!' Unconsciously she twisted around to invite his approval of where she had repinned the cream and gold spray. 'And one other thing so you won't get the ultimate swelled head: I'll grow out of my little infatuation. In fact I can feel myself improving by the minute. Life's been pretty dull around here, and you're astonishingly aggressive!'

'I'm calm enough at the minute,' he said with deceptive mildness. 'I can't promise you I will be when we meet again, but right now I have a house full of guests. Reckless, quick-tempered little females usually go right over my knee!'

She flashed on him one emotion-laden glance and almost flew for the door. Though his voice and manner was cool and authoritative there was a faint trace of violence in the set of his head and tall, powerful body. Men like Brant Elliot were born to give a woman hell, even if it was like Paradise to be locked in his arms, aware of nothing but the touch of his mouth and his hands. If Lori's emotional awakening, at twenty, had been delayed, she knew now she was going to suffer for it. Could there be any greater anguish than loving such a hard, commanding man? A man, moreover, who could choose any woman he wanted, from a formidable list.

Half running, she found the door that led back into the hallway. People were standing there laughing and talking, and Lori turned and at that moment saw Dean. The sight of his thin, sensitive face was more reassuring than she could have ever thought. Even as she was making her way towards him he was rushing forward to meet her, his blue eyes probing for the reason behind the strange radiance that still clung to her, making her more beautiful and more feminine than he had ever seen her.

'Darling, I haven't had a moment's peace since you went off with Elliot!'

'He wanted to show me the rest of the house, but never mind that. I feel like a swim. What about you?'

'Why not?' Dean nodded, pleased. 'A little bit of gossip has been racketing around in your absence. I overheard the Senator say Jane will be changing her name to Elliot any day now!'

'How did he say it, just casually or what?' Lori demanded, half crazy with shock.

'As if he knew what he was talking about,' Dean said abruptly, and took her arm. Brant had come through to the hallway looking so instantly classifiable as a big-time success that Dean was launched into a bitter wave of jealousy. He could hardly fail to be aware that Lori was trembling beneath his hand and he didn't care for the trend of his own thoughts. Lori belonged to him and there were plenty of women Elliot could fascinate. His selection of a wife was already premeditated and purposeful.

Dean led Lori away, almost clicking his tongue. Elliot was a ruthless devil, a man of driving ambition. Poor little Lori could only get hurt by contact.

CHAPTER SIX

FOR almost a week after Dianne walked round in a jealous rage, the reason for which was no secret to Lori. Ever since the night of the party Lori had led a thankless life acting as a buffer between Uncle Viv and his considerably overwrought and therefore highly irritable daughter. Without waiting for any kind of replies Dianne would rattle on for hours about Jane Gifford's limitations, fretting and fuming that she should be so close to Brant while Dianne who wanted his treasured friendship should dwell in the shadows. Jane wasn't an acknowledged beauty like Dianne. She was 'many years' older and for the time being she had drawn all Dianne's considerable venom. Lori, no longer considered a competitor, merely had to bear all the jealous storming for the hours she found herself indoors. Open quarrels were rare while Dianne wore on with her real and imaginary resentments, and it was a lot easier to listen than to contradict. Anyway, Lori believed in her heart that Jane still loved her cousin, whether his return feeling was low key or not. If Jane had once wound herself around his heart, it was his head now that wouldn't let her go. Jane would make Brant an excellent wife and despite Dianne's vehement denigrations she had certain graces Dianne completely lacked.

All that week Lori strove to make her world fall into shape again by working. So determined was she that Albie was never seen to sit in a corner whittling away his surprisingly clever little animal sculptures that he afterwards passionately polished and gave away to every child that came his way for miles around the countryside. The drought was wearing on and fear of an outbreak of bush fires weighed gloomily on all of them. The small town of Madigan a hundred and twenty miles to the south-west had only been spared because the chain of bush fires that threatened it had changed direction at the last moment when the town had been evacuated and all hope given up. What the suffering earth needed was a great downpour, when they were cursed with brilliantly fine days and a dangerous dry wind.

The promised dinner party up at Brant's house had to be cancelled as well, for Brant had decided to harvest the cotton crop as quickly as possible. He had successfully beaten the insect pest menace; now the crop was threatened by drought. If he delayed any longer it was possible most of his fields under cultivation could go up in flames. By the end of the week an army of huge mechanical picking machines had moved in to pull the fluffy white fibre from the open bolls and Brant had no time or inclination for social occasions. Unhappy, neglected Dianne didn't know how to take it, but Lori felt a great sense of reprieve that contrasted vividly with her dreamtime yearning. Her mind she tried hard to control, the heart within her body was something else again. Her physical longing became sharper than ever and she had to fight not to recall the ravishing strength of his arms, the silhouette of his dark head bent above her, the hard mouth, so beautifully, so definitely cut, lowered to hers ... In sleep it possessed her and in the morning when she woke up, tears streaked her face. A climate of danger and excitement surrounded Brant and she had recklessly tempted him as if he were an uncomplicated boy. It had been the greatest mistake of her life and too late now to escape the consequences.

It was a quite different thing with Dean. These days, instead of staying at home practising and committing scores to memory, he came over often with offers to help out. Lori didn't have the heart to refuse his well-meant assistance, but Dean had no flair for horsemanship, mustering or even leading Tilly out of the scrub. For all the good he did he might just as well have stayed at home, and Albie, growing overtired and tense, had been driven to yell that at him in the language most natural to him. Dean had been terribly affronted, and Lori had quite a job pacifying him. She couldn't as Dean suggested 'sack the disgusting old goat!' Albie could go long stretches without pay and if he wasn't remarkably active he was remarkably loyal. Anyway, she couldn't help liking him no matter what. At least Albie spoke plainly and he would never have a catastrophic effect on any woman.

The morning came that Uncle Viv had to be admitted to hospital and Lori had to steel herself not to cry. Uncle Viv sat out on the veranda and slowly smoked a cigarette as if it was the last one he was going to have, while inside Lori put a few things together for him in a bag. It had been decided she would take Uncle Viv into the Junction and Dianne would remain home to mind the farm. Uncle Viv had received the news apparently without interest. There was a stillness about him these days as though his thoughts were constantly turned inwards. Besides, they both knew Dianne had a pathological fear of illness and the atmosphere of a hospital 'positively upset her'.

From time to time Lori cast anxious glances out towards the veranda, but Uncle Viv was sitting quite calmly, without the pentness she had surprised in him the night before. She suppressed her fears again and snapped the bag shut. They had plenty of time to get in to the hospital, but the waiting was unbearable.

Dianne came to the bedroom door and spoke without ceremony. 'Haven't you finished yet?'

Lori shrugged. 'Take it easy!'

'How can I?' Dianne asked scornfully. 'What's the matter with Dad? He doesn't even seem to want to talk to me.'

'Could be he has lots of things on his mind. Can't you at least come in with us?'

Dianne looked at her cousin and her dark eyes were desperate. 'We went into all that last night. You know how I feel about hospitals. They really shake me up. I was there when Mamma died.' She shivered as though she was swept with real terror and Lori said quickly:

'All right, don't upset yourself. If you can't do it, you can't do it, and your father understands you.'

'I expect he does!' Dianne said, and moistened her dry mouth. 'I thought this was going to be a holiday for me, but instead it's turning into hell!'

'You could go back to Sydney again in a few weeks,' Lori suggested, but her cousin laughed contemptuously.

'You'd like that, wouldn't you? I cramp your style. What's to prevent you, for instance, from throwing yourself on Brant's tender mercies? Poor little Lori, trying to manage the farm all on her own! I notice you play that one up a lot!'

'That doesn't even deserve an answer,' Lori said quietly.

'If you had any real go in you you'd get out and take a job!' Dianne burst out wrathfully. 'Surely you've got enough intelligence to know the farm has to be sold up. What Dad has done in the past he can do no longer. I haven't interfered before, but I'm going to interfere now. I'm going to insist that Dad sells out!'

'Then I hope you'll delay that until he's home again. He's in low enough spirits now.'

Dianne's wide, thin shoulders sagged. 'Poor Dad!'

'Come out with me and say goodbye,' said Lori. 'We've got plenty of time, but it's hard to endure the waiting around. I'll drive in fairly slowly.'

Dianne nodded her blonde head, a faint trace of shame on her beautiful chiselled features. 'I just hope all these tests prove Doctor Edmonds an old fool!'

They moved together through the wide, cool hallway and through the open door they saw the swirl of dust from a moving vehicle. It was coming up very fast and as they moved out on to the veranda Brant's big dark green station wagon swept into sight.

Uncle Viv groped for the sides of his chair and stood up, a thin veil of colour coming into his face. 'Has Brant heard I'm going in today?' he asked.

'As far as I'm concerned Brant knows everything,' Lori said involuntarily.

Uncle Viv beamed and Dianne abruptly changed direction. 'You don't suppose he means to take you in?'

'Surely he's too busy?' Uncle Viv protested. 'But it's very kind of him to call all the same.'

Lori turned and gazed out over the shimmering landscape. Through the gaps in the trees they could see the station wagon slashing along the dirt track. The rampant bougainvilleas were so brilliant in the sunlight they dazzled the eye and the big water tanks glinted silver, creating the curious illusion of floating lakes. She was feeling so sick and anxious inside she was almost prepared to let Brant take over in his usual masterful fashion. Lori looked back at Dianne and caught the sudden pleasure in her face. The quality of excited anticipation. The dark eyes shone with a new light and there was colour over her high cheekbones. Lori had never seen such a give-away face and she rigorously schooled her own.

It took Brant a total of two minutes to pull in at the front stairs and he swung out immediately, tall and strong and somehow immensely reassuring. Dianne flew down the steps like a gazelle to greet him and he put his arm around her waist to lead her back up to her father.

'How goes it, Viv? Lori?' The sea-coloured eyes just barely included Lori in their glance.

'I'm going to be all right!' Uncle Viv said brightly as the two men shook hands. 'Edmonds is an old fuss-pot.'

'I think so too!' Dianne added with a touch of resentment.

Lori said nothing and Brant replied mildly: 'Well, it won't hurt you to take his advice. You've got to rest a little, Viv, and get that leg right. If you're ready to go I'd like to run you in. It's a comfort to have a man around even if you have got two beautiful girls to hold your hand!'

Lori was almost paralysed by Dianne's quick volte-face. She smiled and nodded encouragement, taking her father's arm and pressing it. 'Isn't that lovely! Now we can go in in comfort. It's so much easier travelling in an air-conditioned car!'

'Look here, Brant,' Uncle Viv spoke in a gratified voice, 'you're much too busy to bother about me. I'll make it with Lori's help.'

'And *mine*!' Dianne stressed a shade frantically.

'Honestly, darling, Lori's so possessive sometimes I can't even reach my own father!' Her lovely face mirrored her great concern while the dark eyes challenged anyone to contradict.

Brant looked unhurriedly from one to the other, then he said with automatic authority, 'This is something I'd like to do, Viv. After all, we're good friends and neighbours and the men can manage for a while without me. We've everything under control anyway.'

'That's marvellous!' Uncle Viv said, and picked up his bag composedly. 'Thanks, little Lori. You know darn well I couldn't manage without you!'

'Well, you've got *me* to take you into the Junction!' Dianne told him now. 'Lori can stay home and look after the farm. She's always so anxious, poor thing. It's so sweet of you, Brant, to want to help us!'

Brant turned to Lori, his brilliant eyes cool. 'Are you coming or staying?' he asked.

'It looks as if I'm staying. I'll phone through to check on Uncle Viv this afternoon and of course I'll be visiting him.'

'Don't worry, darling,' Dianne said breezily, 'we'll manage without you. It makes a lot of difference to me to have Dad to myself.'

They all turned and walked down to the car, and at the last moment Uncle Viv put his bag down and took Lori into his arms, dropping a kiss into her bright hair. 'Thank you, Lori. I had something to tell you, but I'll tell you tomorrow.'

She thought she wouldn't cry, but the tears sprang into her eyes. 'Take care, dear. I'll ring you!'

Beside them Dianne gave a funny mock groan. 'Don't get all emotional on us, Lori. Dad's only going in for a check-up!'

Lori swallowed her prayer, but she went right

ahead and hugged her uncle's tall, spare frame while he patted her shoulder as if it was she who was in need of comfort.

Brant took charge of the overnight bag and stowed it away in the rear compartment while Dianne slid across the front seat so she could sit beside him. There was plenty of room for Uncle Viv in front as well and Lori helped him in, hurriedly blinking back her tears. It had to be her reaction to strain, because she felt as if she was truly saying goodbye to her dearest relative. It was more than a feeling; it was a dreadful apprehensiveness. She saw her uncle's face in close-up, Dianne beside him looking almost radiant when she had no right. She put up her hand in salute and moved away from the car, lifting her eyes to Brant standing outside the driver's side.

'I'm grateful, Brant. Thanks a lot!'

His eyes skimmed her small slender figure, seeing the valiant way she was keeping back her tears. 'I'll check with you later, just to reassure myself.'

'We'll be all right, really!'

She wanted to ward him off and he knew it. His dark face went hard and taut and without another word he swung into the car and turned on the engine. Lori withdrew into the shade, conscious of the suffocating beat of her heart. As the big car came around Uncle Viv waved almost gravely, with Dianne beside him looking for all the world as if she was going on a pleasure excursion. Brant didn't wave at all and Lori supposed she deserved it. It was easy for her these days to recognise the anger in him. He might think her gauche and ungrateful, but then he had no idea what sort of person Dianne was. Lori knew the older girl's bewildering moods only too well and she had no wish to encourage them. Dianne was one of those women who couldn't stand a man paying attention to anyone but herself, and when it came to Brant she was quite obsessive.

Lori watched until the station wagon was out of sight, then she walked slowly back into the house, feeling absolutely bereft. She shook her head as though it was as heavy as her heart, then with deliberation she went into her bedroom and changed her simple yellow sun-frock for her working clothes, jeans and a cotton shirt. Albie wouldn't work well without her and there was always so much to do. Dianne *was* right—she was fighting a losing battle and very nearly fighting it alone. All that was important now was the state of Uncle Viv's health. Five minutes later when she left the house it occurred to her to wonder what it was Uncle Viv wanted to tell her. It must have been private, otherwise he would have told her there and then. Ah well, he would tell her in his own good time. She whistled up the dogs, drowsing heavily in the shade, and within seconds they came racing towards her in a full charge, hesitating right at her feet when they came smartly to attention, tongues lolling, tails wagging, eyeing her with bright intelligent eyes.

'Right-oh!' she said briskly. 'Tory, you find Albie. Rex, you come with me!'

Both dogs seemed to grin at her as though they had been offered a special treat, then Tory went off in search of Albie while Lori went to saddle up the mare.

It was mid-afternoon when Lori got her first whiff of smoke. For a moment she didn't know which direction it was coming from. There were no birds in the vicinity to warn her, and that was a bad sign. No part of the day had gone according to plan. She had returned to the house a little later than midday expecting to find Dianne home, but there was no sign that she had even returned to the house. Albie for some reason had disappeared with the mare and she still didn't know his whereabouts, and if that wasn't enough one of the cows was making distressed sounds from deep in the bush.

Lori moved cautiously ahead leading Smoky, Uncle Viv's ageing grey, carefully around fallen branches and sticks that might crack under hoof and frighten the beast further into the scrub. It was hard going with Smoky when once it had been a beautiful mover and she didn't like to press the animal in the heat.

The whiff of smoke emphatically changed her plans. She lifted her head, horse and rider, sniffing at the air. The only good thing about it, there was no breeze. A fire could travel quickly with a breeze. She swallowed nervously, adrenalin pumping into her blood. If it was fire, what could she do? For a frozen instant she even saw flames whipping round her. A big fire had been raging on Barradon for days, but so far it hadn't crossed the range. Sitting on the veranda last night she and Uncle Viv had reached the conclusion that it would burn itself out, but Lori remembered vividly now the bright glow spreading across the dark purple sky. In the heat of the day that same fire would burn far more intensely.

Swiftly she turned Smoky's head around, sighing and steeling herself against the piteous sounds coming from the grey-green wall of scrub. She couldn't do anything about it now. She had to get back to high ground and check on that ominous drift of smoke. If there was a small outbreak and a wind got up it could sweep across the run and threaten the house.

By the time she broke out into clear ground, the gelding was nearly staggering and a great wave of fear

assailed Lori as she saw a great torrent of smoke belch
out of the trees. The shock of it affected her violently
and the horse that seemed ready to drop began to act
up in its fear. Even as she watched, the scarlet tongues
of flame leapt up from the smoke and the sap in the
gum leaves and the oily-barked branches exploded
into blazing crackles, firing the grass.

For the first time it came to her she could die.
Everything could go—the house and the cattle, the
horses and dogs, the small bush creatures that re-
garded the farm as their sanctuary. The great gum
tree that had stood on the property for more years
than anyone could remember was now a funeral pyre,
burning savagely. Any sudden wind could bring it
down on her, roaring across the grass. She began to
shout for Albie at the top of her voice, holding in the
terrified horse, while black crows like omens streaked
out across the sky, flying noisily towards the creeks,
and hawks in droves bombarded the legions of lizards
and insects that scuttled from the blaze.

It was apparent now that the fire was beating down
her way, running in a parallel line to the creek. Heat
whirlwinds had sprung up, carrying strips of flaming
bark a hundred yards or more down to the parched
flats that licked up immediately. There were breaks
burned all around the house and the holding yards,
but unless the fire changed direction, it was burning
away from the house and down towards the green
river gums.

Smoky was struggling violently, slobbering from
the mouth, and out of the scrub raced bellowing
strays, thundering down the slope to safety. The only
thing Lori could do was follow them, to keep ahead of
the inferno, for it might never cross the creek. Fear

was twisting round like a mad thing inside her, but she fought to keep herself under control. A breeze was fanning up now, bringing down the greedy licks of flame from the trees, sweeping across the crackling grass so her ears seemed filled with the sound of it, and her eyes full of billowing smoke.

It was incredible, the speed and ferocity of the fire's progress, the razed earth humming to its crackling roar. She was shaking uncontrollably, crouched down low on the gelding's neck, forcing it harder and harder. It seemed to be moving so slowly and she could feel the unbearable heat of the swirling, advancing fire at her back. She tried to speak to the poor straining animal, but the smoke made her cough. It was becoming thicker, filling her lungs. In another minute she would scream with mindless panic. They were in a frightful plight and Smoky didn't seem able to bear her weight, unwillingly condemning them both to death.

Please God! Lori cried out in silent agony. Please help me!

Her fear now was that Smoky would drop dead beneath her. The heavily timbered line of the creek loomed up before her, green as an oasis in the parched land, then forcing itself upon her realisation, away to the right, a small convoy of trucks making their way across the valley coming down over Brant's property. They would be too late! No one could save her now. Smoky was finished, flagging in his distress, and both of them would be incarcerated in the lavishly beautiful, terrible prison of flame. She could never reach the creek as she might have done with her own mare, and a deathly feeling of acceptance began to transfix her mind. A scorching haze now covered the brazen face

of the sun and she began to whisper brokenly the
names of her loved ones ... snatches of prayer. Surely
someone would answer her?

Out of the pungent, scented smoke before her broke
the bold silhouette of a horse and rider. Unbelie-
vable—but it wasn't her imagination! She saw them
take the boundary fence together in one mighty leap,
then come on right for her, flying into danger. In some
terribly weird detached fashion, she could even appreciate the remarkable display of horsemanship, the
superb turn of speed of the flying, black satin body.
Brant sat astride his magnificent black mare, swinging
low over her neck, digging his heels in, running her
right into the holocaust, not giving her any chance to
unseat him or show her great fear, but covering the
ground in tremendous lengthening strides.

Lori could hear him call to her urgently, but the
words were unintelligible, drowned by the crackling
roar of the fire. For a few seconds the gelding seemed
to respond to the clamour before it, then it almost
buckled, the run gone right out of it. Lori's hat had
long since come off and the only colour about her was
the red-gold of her hair, an ironic glory, for it was the
colour of the flames that threatened to engulf her.

In their race for life, the splendid horse and rider
halted as one alongside her. Brant wheeled the mare's
head around, shouting to her, his nostrils flaring, eyes
blazing, his face the way Lori had never seen it, hewn
out of bronze, so powerful in its cast it might even
dare the flames. She couldn't begin to express her wild
relief, her small face was agonised, streaked with
grime and tears.

'For God's sake, Lori, *let go*!' He grabbed at the
reins and she almost hit his hands away in her
anguish.

'I can't leave the poor thing!'

'God!'

'Oh, Brant!' The hoarse little voice was her own. She was sobbing in great panting gasps, horrified at having to leave her uncle's gallant old horse even when her own life was at stake.

Desperately Brant pulled the mare hard up alongside her and hurtled her bodily out of the saddle and up before him, crushing the very breath from her body.

'Stop that damned racket!' he yelled at her in the fury of the moment. 'You're not going to die, but the poor beast is finished!'

The magnificent mare was rearing now, wild-eyed and giving great snorting gasps of terror, but Brant had her under control within seconds and urged her away from the wall of flame.

Before the flames reached it, the grey gelding was dead and they were galloping straight for the deepest reaches of the creek with the fire in sheets at their backs, singeing their skin and their hair. The anguished cries that floated above the flames were those of the firefighters and volunteers helpless to save them. Brant was holding Lori savagely and she was in so much pain it seemed probable he had cracked her ribs with his powerful grip. She was thrown back against him in a paroxysm of shock and they were rushing downhill hell for leather in an unrestrained gallop ... down the sloping banks of the creek to the listening, whispering, agitated trees.

Lori was conscious of nothing, not even shivering anticipation, as the mare in its overwhelming determination to carry them to safety, gathered itself and flew midstream, plunging them all into deep, foaming water.

She was going to be burned alive. Flames were licking round her, yet they never seemed to hurt her. She felt as if she was raving and she tore at the bonds that held her, and as she did so a low, distinct voice brought her right out of it.

'*Lori!*'

There were terrible weights on her eyes, yet she opened them. Brant was bending over her, his dark face all angles. 'You were having a nightmare!'

'So we're alive, then?' was all she could think of to say. She moved slightly and winced with the pain. It seemed to be all over her body and there were swirling clouds around her head.

'Rest easy!' he said, and held her back gently against the pillows. 'I'm afraid I've bruised you badly and both of us took a crack on the head from a submerged branch, something I couldn't prevent.'

'Where am I?'

'You're here in my house. Where else would you be?'

'The farm!' she said tremulously. 'Please tell me what's happened? Dianne and Albie and ... *everything!*'

His mouth thinned just slightly at the panic and fear, then he said slowly, 'Both of them are quite safe. At the moment you're under sedation and when you wake again properly we'll have a little talk. You don't have a thing to worry about. *Nothing!*' As he spoke he soothed her forehead gently and despite herself her eyes began to close again. She was dimly aware that he had pulled up a chair to the side of her bed but the swirling clouds of unconsciousness were coming for her again.

The next time Lori came round, Jane was in the chair

by her bed watching her with concern.

'There now, you're awake! How do you feel?'

Lori's enormous amber eyes filled with weak tears and Jane stood up instantly, making sympathetic noises. 'Poor little girl! What a terrible time you've had!'

Lori shook her head. 'I'd be dead but for Brant. Was he really beside me during the night, or did I dream it?'

Jane stopped straightening the pillows and looked down at her and smiled. 'Brant is like that. He only went off to snatch a few hours' sleep a little while ago. You don't remember Doctor Edmonds being here?'

'No.'

'Well, he was. He's going to look in again some time this afternoon. We thought at first you might have cracked a few ribs, but it proved to be very bad bruising. I daresay you'll be black and blue when they come fully out. You're only a fragile little thing really and I suppose Brant had to use a lot of force.'

'I won't hold it against him!' Lori said quietly. 'How is he? He seemed just the same when he spoke to me.'

'Indestructible!' Jane said with a smile in her grey eyes.

'You care for him very much, don't you?' Lori said, lying back on her pillows.

'Of course I do!' Jane confirmed warmly. 'Brant is absolutely dynamic, a tower of strength!'

Lori could only second that, though some lancelike little pain stabbed at her heart. Jane was a lovely woman, kind and compassionate. She could hardly hold it against her that she had always been an important part of Brant's life. The sooner she got up and went home again the better.

'Did Doctor Edmonds say when I could get up?' she asked quickly, and Jane looked her astonishment.

'Just a minute, young lady, you're not going anywhere. Not for a day or two at least. You need looking after.'

'It's kind of you, Jane, but I must see what's happened to the farm. Uncle Viv left me in charge. Now I scarcely know how to tell him.'

Jane's smile pulled a little strangely. 'Give yourself a little time to regain your strength. Your cousin, I understand, is staying with the Camfields and your man, Albie, is looking after the farmhouse. Mercifully it wasn't touched by the fire and it burned out at the creekline with a little bit of help. It seemed like a miracle that Brant was home to alert everyone. He could so easily have been elsewhere, and Mother and I would have been frantic wondering what to do and who to call. Thank God you both emerged safely. I believe quite a few people were sick watching. It was a close call!'

'And Black Magic?' Lori held her breath.

'She swam downstream and came out on the other side. Quite the heroine!'

'I'm so glad! Brant really loves her!' Lori's small face was brooding, but a little colour had come into it. 'This beautiful nightdress must be yours.' She caught her lower lip between her teeth and looked down at the exquisite palest cream satin and lace nightgown. 'I've never worn such a beautiful thing in my life!'

'Well, I must say it suits you,' Jane said soothingly. 'I just had to tie it on the shoulder so it wouldn't come off. Your cousin is bringing over a few things for you so you'll feel more comfortable.'

'Did she tell you if our two dogs are all right?'

'Yes, dear!' Jane said quickly. 'I understand they

were with your man, Albie. They were working to the back of the property, so they mercifully survived. Albie is asking to see you. He was terribly upset and not all that easy to control, but Brant promised him he could call in for a moment later on today.'

Lori closed her eyes for a minute, getting the after-vision of Jane's tall elegant figure, the smooth sweep of her fair hair. 'I'm very grateful to you, Jane, for trying to help me. I can see in your face how kind you are, but I must go home. Believe me, I'll be all right and Dianne will be there!' She pressed a hand to her aching body and said more strongly, 'Besides, I must speak to Uncle Viv. Someone has to break the news to him gently. It can't be kept from him for long and I'd rather he hear it from me. This will drive us out, you see. The farm is finished.'

There was some slight desperation in Jane's fine grey eyes. 'Please, dear, at least wait until Brant speaks to you. You really are in no condition to get up and Doctor Edmonds gave orders that you stay there. Promise me you'll rest quietly until Brant sees you. I'll be in a panic if you don't!' She was standing beside the bedside table and her soft voice was urgent.

'Then it's a promise!' Lori said simply, and half raised herself on her pillows. 'You mustn't pamper me, Jane, I'm not used to it.'

'It seems to me, dear, you're worn out!' Jane gave the young girl in the bed a kind and curious look. 'You're not at all like your cousin, are you? I was speaking to her only this morning.'

'What did she say?'

'She was naturally very upset.'

Lori pondered on this, trying to pinpoint some elusive quality in Jane's voice and manner, looking up at the older woman with brilliant amber eyes, her tender mouth sad. 'Poor Dianne! This hasn't been much of a time for her—her father being ill and now this! At least it will bring matters to a head. The problems with the farm have been never-ending. Too much work and not enough money. Uncle Viv won't be able to bear the strain. For once I'll have to agree with Dianne—we'll have to sell out and find a little peace and quiet. I suppose Albie will know the stock loss.'

Jane went to the door and stood there, the coral of her dress reflected in the brightness of her mouth. 'I don't like you to worry any more. I know you have a lot of faith in Brant, Lord knows I have enough of it in him myself—wait until he talks the whole situation over with you. I'm going to get your breakfast now. You'll feel better when you've eaten.'

'Thanks, Jane,' Lori said with a softened expression. 'But remember now, I'm not an invalid. I'll get up just as soon as I've spoken to Brant.'

'We'll see!' Jane said rapidly, and disappeared, leaving Lori with the strangest notion that there had been the faintest glistening of tears in the fine grey eyes. She smoothed her fingers over the finest cotton sheet noticing how roughened they were, though the hands themselves were small and finely boned, then she thought of all the wasted effort, the sheer back-breaking hard work. Poor Uncle Viv, he would be terribly distressed when he heard the news. She only prayed God it hadn't been broken to him, though no one responsible would inflict sudden shock on a sick man. Fire, on the very day he went to hospital. It didn't seem possible, yet it had kept him out of danger. Lori lay back on her pillows, caught up in her anxieties. Would anything ever come right again?

A few minutes later there was a tap on the door and

Dianne almost burst into the room. She walked quickly across the golden stretch of carpet and stared down at the girl in the bed.

'It's all your rotten fault!' she declared wildly, a spasmodic tic under her right eye. 'You knew Dad was ill, but you kept on and on about the beastly farm. You've robbed me of my father, and I could *kill* you!'

Even as she spoke she jerked at Lori with strong hands, her face appallingly white and cords of tension standing up in her long, graceful neck. 'I think it's time for you to know like the rest of us. Dad's dead— yes, *dead*. He suffered a fatal heart attack. Some fool from the valley got through to him at the hospital and told him the farm was alight. The Sister didn't get there quick enough to cut off the call. It took him just an hour to die, and you lie here breathing. I could kill you!'

Shock and horror transfixed Lori's expression. She didn't even feel Dianne's hurting hands. 'It can't be true!' she whispered.

Dianne's voice swelled to a cry. 'It is, damn you. *It is!*' She put her hand to Lori's tousled hair and pulled it savagely, much as she had done years before in an argument. 'Come on, get up and come home. It's bad, bad, news, but first I'm going to tell you . . .'

She was caught up by a swift interruption. Brant stood in the open doorway with Jane and her mother hovering anxiously at his shoulder, their faces quivering with dismay. 'You're a wonderful person in a sickroom!' Brant said curtly. 'Come away from the bed, Dianne!'

'Oh yes,' she cried bitterly, 'by all means protect little Lori. She needs cherishing. Aren't you jealous, Jane? There are a few things you ought to know about this treacherous little redhead!'

Brant glanced back quickly at the two women. 'I don't want you to hear or see any of this!'

'Of course!' Mrs Trevelyan said almost calmly, and took her daughter's arm. 'We'll wait for you in the living room.'

'What a nice life!' Dianne called after them, almost ugly in her grief and her anger.

Lori thought she would never get her strength back again, yet somehow she slipped out of the bed. Dianne was really crying now and her breathing was harsh and painful. With complete abstraction Lori reached for the matching peignoir Jane had left lying over the arm of a chair, but Brant took it from her and held it while she slipped her arms with a curious listlessness into the sleeves.

'Are you all right?' he asked, looking down at her stilled face.

'Don't worry!'

Her whispered tones reached Dianne's tortured ears. 'Don't bother about me, Brant. I'm only the bereaved daughter. Why worry about me?'

'I am worried about you,' he said quietly. 'Try to pull yourself together or you'll make yourself ill!'

She looked up at him and the tears streaked her pale face. 'I've lost my mother, now my father! Why can't people live for ever?' A spasm ran through her slender body and she put her head down on her arms, wailing as though her heart would break.

Brant's voice seemed to come to Lori from afar off. 'You've got to lie down, or sit down or something. Here, Lori!' His hands were there to guide her into an armchair, but her great eyes fixed themselves on him unseeingly. There seemed to be a great icy barrier between her and the outside world. Even Brant.

'Go on, Brant,' Dianne lifted her head to taunt him.

'Hold her hand. I'm utterly crushed, but all your concern is for Lori. It's been like that ever since I can remember. The people I care about always seem to care about Lori. Maybe it's the baby curls or the false air of fragility. I happen to know she's as strong as a horse!'

Brant looked at her briefly and something in his expression brought colour into Dianne's whitened cheeks. 'I know how you're feeling, Dianne, and believe me I share your grief, but it will be so much better if you sit quietly and not try to further upset yourself or your cousin. You're both badly shocked, but Lori is physically weakened. She's been living on her reserves for quite a while now. I'm sure your father would want you to be kind to her!'

'Oh, bless you, Brant!' Dianne said with a bitter smile. 'Dad left me everything he had. I suppose he would have got around to changing his will what with Lori doing her level best to cut me out, but the fact is he hadn't made a new will for twenty years, so it all comes to me. Name your price and I'll sell out. You probably won't want it anyway. It looks like the near side of hell!'

'Leave all that for the right time and the right place!' Brant returned curtly, his brilliant blue-green gaze moving over Dianne's tense face. 'I understood you were coming with a few things for Lori, now it seems you came to attack her!'

'You don't know how I'd like to!' Dianne said slowly, giving him a most peculiar glance. 'You seem to be taking a little too much interest in Lori for your own good. What does Jane have to say about it, or doesn't she suspect anything?'

Brant stood up abruptly, tall and strikingly formidable. 'Your time has just run out. Gavin is waiting

outside in the car for you. Whatever I can do to help
you, I will, but I won't listen to any more of your talk.
If you'll allow me I'll attend to the funeral arrangements and take that burden off your shoulders and we
can talk later about what you want to do with the
property. I haven't the heart for it right at the
moment.'

Dianne watched his face without speaking, then she
got up in one convulsive movement. 'My only wish is
to get as far away from here as possible, and I do think
you might spare Lori. I need her company. Naturally
I won't see her penniless.'

'Naturally!' Brant returned suavely, and his handsome mouth thinned. 'Allow me to see you out.'

'And what about Lori?' Dianne demanded. 'When
is she coming home?'

'When she's well enough,' Brant said positively.
'You're staying with the Camfields, aren't you?'

'Any objection?' said Dianne, flushed and dangerous.

'Not at all. They seem to trust you. It may well be
they want to buy the property themselves.'

'As a matter of fact we've already discussed it!'
Dianne said with a kind of cold fury. 'They seem to
think you should have the first option. Honestly,
everyone is so in *favour* of you, Brant!' She paused
and looked down at Lori, sitting so small and withdrawn. 'When you're ready to come home, let me
know. If you had any pride at all, you'd leave now.
We've things to discuss, and you're not such a fool
that you won't listen!'

Lori looked up at her and there were hollows under
her cheekbones and in her delicate throat. 'I'm so
sorry, Dianne. If you need me I'll come now.'

'I'm afraid not!' Brant said imperiously, towering

over both of them. 'You can go home in a few days' time, Lori. If you still want to.'

Dianne's dark eyes glittered, but whatever sprang into her mind she hesitated to say. 'All right, then,' she said shortly, 'I'll let you cry your heart out in private. I won't be going to the funeral. I just couldn't bear it!' She began to cry drearily again and Lori pulled herself to her feet, overcome with compassion. Brant turned back to her and the expression in his eyes was so intense and authoritative she felt helpless to even get past him. The hand outstretched towards Dianne fell numbly to her side and she saw Brant put his arm around Dianne and lead her through the door while she clung to him in a mixture of passion and anguish.

For a few seconds Lori stood dazed and bereft, then she walked back to the bed and quietly passed out.

CHAPTER SEVEN

DURING the next three days Lori never left Brant's house except for the funeral, that was attended by nearly everyone in the district. Mrs Camfield had somehow persuaded Dianne to go and she had been supported by the entire Camfield clan. It was one of the hottest days anyone had ever known, and that same afternoon great storm clouds built up in the south and advanced across the valley, absorbing everyone's interest until they could think of nothing except that now at least they just might get some rain.

Only Lori looked up at the darkening sky and eyed it with a kind of bitter anger. She heard the rumbling thunder, the almost forgotten chorus of frogs, breaking the dreadful stillness of the day; she saw the vivid flashes of lightning that even that moment were illuminating the barren, blackened farm, and still the tears wouldn't come. She had lost all interest in everything. Even the rain.

Nearly everyone in the valley was out waiting to catch the first drops of rain in their hands, though the earth and sky were seemingly being torn asunder by the savage intensity of the storm's buildup, and the rolling, shifting heavens were an indescribable volcanic colour, purple and black and a virulent green with incredibly bright shafts of sunlight vying with the gigantic silver electrical probes.

Jane and her mother, unused to the terrific storms and somehow excluded from the rain fever, had taken shelter inside the house, but Lori was too tautly strung to join them. She stood on the veranda unmoved by the brilliantly eerie spectacle, the unleashed elemental power, thinking that now when Uncle Viv's life was over, the rain would come.

Another vivid streak of lightning lit up the sky, followed by a tremendous crash of thunder, and she felt like lifting her small fist to the sky and calling: 'Exultant cruel gods, how you laugh at us!'

Instead she stood there very quietly while the first drops fell heavily, big and isolated, spattering the roof and the paths and the garden, causing the frogs to croak more excitedly and the parrots to screech loudly calling an end to their sufferings. The searing heat of the day was falling dramatically and those first heralding drops turned almost instantly into a steady deluge. Now at last the fires would halt. Now the ranges would turn amethyst again and the green grass would spring up lusher and longer than ever. All the birds would return and the buzzing mosquitoes, but she couldn't get her grief out of her mind.

Someone came to stand behind her, taking her shoulders, trying to ease the tension out of them. 'Come away, Lori, you're getting wet!'

'It's rain, Brant,' she insisted. 'Can't you feel it?'

The touch of his hands was twisting something deep inside her, calling up emotions she didn't want to feel. She broke away from him almost in a panic and ran down the short flight of steps out into the fragrantly incensed garden, her legs weak and shaky, holding up her face to the glorious rain. It washed all over her, soaking her to the skin, darkening the shining red-gold of her hair. Real rain. The life-giver. Rain they had waited for for so long. Even then it released something in her and her small face contorted abruptly. After their time of tribulation, this! What a tragedy Uncle Viv couldn't see it. The thought made her want to stand screaming in the rain, but Brant was there gathering her into his arms while she let her aching head fall against his hard chest.

'Cry, Lori,' he ordered a little harshly. 'It would be the best thing for you!'

It didn't occur to her to question why she turned to him instinctively. All she was conscious of was the thud of his heart and the steady drumming of the rain. Nothing was clear to her now. She felt painfully helpless, unconvinced whether crying would make her feel better or not. In the pouring rain she half lay against him as though it was comforting to be held against his wet, strong body, letting her mind drift, for before too long she had to make a life of her own. All she had done counted for nothing. Uncle Viv had left the farm to his own and she accepted it. Perhaps if he had lived he might have made provision for her, but she was young and she had a few accomplishments and she wasn't frightened of making her own way. The hand that shaped her nape was almost a caress and she stirred to look up into Brant's darkly sculptured face glistening with rain water, his thick black hair curling crisply round his head.

'Oh, God, Brant,' she whispered, 'I'm so unhappy.'

'Yes, I know.' He held her chin deliberately and dropped a brief hard kiss on her mouth. 'Come here to me, you're shivering!'

He lifted her like a feather weight and carried her in out of the pouring rain, while everywhere across the valley people went delirious with joy.

It was another two days before Lori felt capable of returning to the farm. Brant had gone into the Junction on an early morning appointment, and it was this more than anything that made Lori's decision. In the first shock of her grief she had forgotten Jane. Not that Jane and Mrs Trevelyan hadn't been kindness itself to her, but she told herself firmly she had to go home. It was time to deal with her difficulties herself. Jane was Brant's chosen woman and she had been in the house long enough to appreciate their wonderful compatibility.

In her room she packed her small case with trembling fingers. One of Brant's men would run her back to the farm. She had only to say goodbye to Jane and her mother. Brant was used to her running away from him. He might be angry, but he would soon realise it was all for the best. After all she wasn't an orphan any longer but a grown woman. Dianne was still safe with the Camfields, but she had made no further effort to contact her cousin. When Lori reached the farm she would have to ring her and find out what Dianne intended to do. She was too sick at heart to consider that one day very soon Brant would probably own the farm as well.

She heard movements outside her door, then a light tap. She called a quick: 'Come in' and Jane stood in the open doorway, her smile turning into a slight frown when she saw what Lori was doing.

'Dearest girl, you're not thinking of leaving us, are you?'

'I must,' Lori said firmly so she wouldn't cry. 'You've done more than enough for me, Jane, and I can't thank you enough. But it's time for me now to pick up my life. I have to see what Dianne intends to do and I have to keep my own self-respect.'

'But surely, dear, you do that, just by being yourself.' Jane crossed the room quickly and put her hand on Lori's shoulder. 'I can see you're determined. Would you like me to come with you? Believe me, dear, I know how you feel. I loved my husband deeply.'

Lori put up her own hand and covered Jane's for a moment. 'I can't subject you to my grief. I'll be all right, really. Albie's there and I want to see Rex and Tory. They'll be missing me.'

'By the way, it almost slipped my mind, your friend Dean is coming over this morning,' Jane informed her.

Lori lifted her case and put it down on the floor. 'Then he can give me a lift over. It feels so odd not to have a home any more.'

Jane scarcely knew what comment to make, so she made none. It seemed obvious that Lori's uncle had been caught unprepared by death, for he couldn't have been so heartless as to leave his niece turned out of the only home she had known since her parents' tragic accident. 'Would you consider coming to stay with us for a while?' she suggested. 'I mean, if you have nowhere in particular to go Mother and I would be delighted to have you with us in Brisbane. We have a lovely little beach house at the Gold Coast, and it's obvious you're badly in need of a holiday.'

Lori looked up, surprised. 'I didn't think you'd be leaving Brant so soon.'

'Well, dear, circumstances dictate our course. I feel I'd really be contributing something if I could help you. I like you and certainly Mother does. Brant won't mind in the least, and now he has the harvest out of the way and more or less on the top of things he can take a well-earned rest himself. You've no idea how difficult it is to persuade him. Bryan's the same, to put it mildly. We were engaged at one time, but I suppose he's well over me by now.'

'Who's Bryan?' Lori asked in blank wonder.

'Why, Brant's elder brother,' Jane explained apologetically. 'Hasn't Brant ever spoken of him?'

'No.'

Jane threw back her head and crowed with laughter. 'How ridiculous! The pair of them are normally very garrulous about one another. If you come to stay with us, and it would be simply lovely if you would, you'll certainly be meeting Bryan. He handles all my business affairs, so to speak. Very well, I might add. I'm every bit as simple as he seems to think. Brant's much more tolerant, but they're both dynamos. I grew up with them, don't forget.'

The conversation, though unfinished, had to be left right there, for Mrs Trevelyan came to the door, her expression vaguely troubled when she saw Lori's packed case. 'Your friend is here, Lori. He's waiting in the living room.' She glanced at her daughter, then down towards Lori's case. 'This child isn't leaving us, surely?'

'We must let her do what she thinks best,' Jane said simply. 'Being fond of her as we are, I've asked her to stay with us when we go back to Brisbane. A few weeks of being cosseted seem in order!'

'Yes indeed,' Mrs Trevelyan agreed gently. 'You can be very sure of your welcome, Lori, but it's possible Brant might have other ideas. We must talk to him about it. For one, he's very concerned about your welfare and it doesn't help to get in his way. Bryan's the same!'

'Never mind,' Jane said, smiling. 'We'll work everything out. Now I expect Dean has come along to offer comfort. He's a perfectly wonderful pianist. He must stir himself to get back to professional life. Such a rare talent can't be wasted.'

The strange thing was that Dean himself repeated

this when they were more than half way to the farm. He had been unexpectedly reserved with Jane and her mother, but so gentle with Lori that she started to wonder why one couldn't love to order. Dean seemed to need her badly and she had nothing to offer him but friendship. If she let him believe anything else she would only succeed in hurting him.

'Now your uncle's gone,' he said, and his sensitive mouth was suddenly obstinate, 'there's nothing to stop you coming away with me. I can't think of anything I want more than to wake up in the morning with you beside me.'

'Please, Dean!' she begged, shaken by the passion in his voice.

'I'm sorry!' he leant over and patted her hand. 'Now is not the time to talk about it, I suppose, but I want you to know how I feel. With you beside me it will be easy to keep my balance. I get so strung up and you're so sweet and tender. You give me peace. It's a musician's job to give himself. I'm used to feeling depleted. But all that would change if I had you. You're so vital I'm beginning to feel desperately insecure without you.'

'I don't love you, Dean,' she said with a quiet certainty.

He didn't answer for a moment. 'You won't escape me, all the same. Let's get a few things straight. Everyone in the valley knows Dianne got the farm—the dear little girl has been broadcasting it around. You're not trained for anything and obviously you have to get married some time. I'm sure I can make you happy. I've always known that.'

Lori's unhappiness, which was very real, was reflected in her face. She had lost weight and the delicate bone structure of her face showed cleanly, the amber eyes shadowed and brilliant with near-tears. Always slight, she was now positively ethereal, and Dean looked at her from under his heavy lashes, filled with a bright, disturbing desire. Despite what she said, Lori would come to love him, and his intensely blue eyes moved over her as if he already had the right to call her his own.

It was quite impossible for Lori to be any kind of company. She paid no real attention to anything Dean was saying, though Jane's invitation had left a deep feeling of relief like a necessary breathing space.

'It's rather confusing,' she said slowly, 'but Jane wasn't engaged to Brant at all. It was his brother.'

'I know that,' Dean answered with a defensive bitterness.

'But you told me . . .'

'Who cares what I told you? I'd do anything to pin you down and marry you.'

She was whiter than white, but she met his eyes squarely. 'What on earth do you mean?'

'Oh, I just had the notion you were falling for Elliot yourself.'

'How strange!' said Lori, her small oval face carved into a delicate mask.

'You mean strange you could fall in love with him?' Dean asked, with a burst of jealousy he couldn't control.

'Brant would never look at me in that way,' she said, and shook her head emphatically.

'No, he's not worth fighting over,' Dean agreed, 'and don't think for a moment he'll keep us apart.'

For a shocked instant Lori covered her face with her hands. She was bewildered by Dean's vengeful attitude and so weakened she felt helpless to combat it. He lifted one hand off the wheel and snatched her hands away from her face, seeing with relief that she wasn't crying.

'I'm sorry, darling, I just lost control. When you're feeling better, we'll talk it over. You know quite well you must do something, and that something is marry me. Mother will get over the shock, and if she doesn't she'll have to remember I'm the one with the talent.' The strong, elegant hand tightened over Lori's shoulder, then went back to the wheel.

Lori was voiceless, shifting her glittering gaze to the intolerably blackened farm. In spite of herself she began to shake uncontrollably. Mentally she had prepared herself for black desolation, but nothing could exceed the intensity of reality. Here fire had raged, burning countless trees sweeping right down to the creek where it had been halted by the lack of grass and an army of determined firefighters. Dean kept driving in silence and she blinked her eyes repeatedly, refusing to break down. All they had worked for—gone, gone away on the wind.

Dean parked the car in the shade of the bougain-villeas and even as they were walking to the house, Albie came out, red-eyed and none too sober.

'Mornin', Miss Lori,' he said in a quiet, dignified way, then apparently in an outburst of rage, 'What's this young feller doin' 'ere?'

Dean froze in indignation. 'Mind your own damned business.'

'Lookin' after Miss Lori is my business,' Albie said, very belligerently for him.

'Don't make a fuss, Albie,' said Lori, walking towards him. 'I don't think I could stand it!'

Albie appeared to give way with a fair amount of tolerance, his saddened smile a little rueful. 'S'pose

I'm just plain miserable. Least you look a bit better than the last time I seen yah!'

'Thanks for looking after the house, Albie,' Lori said thankfully. 'Where are the dogs?'

'Ya don't 'ave to worry about them,' Albie assured her. 'They were 'ere this mornin' when I waved me 'ands. Reckon they're down at the creek now. Life's just one big laugh after the rains. 'Course they're missin' the boss,' he added gloomily, and looked down at the ground. 'Reckon I am too!'

He looked so lost and listless, his big hands incessantly twitching, that Lori suggested he take the day off and go into town, even when it was fairly evident where he would be heading. Albie had been on the property for almost twenty years and his misery and dejection was understandable. 'You can take the utility,' Lori offered, then remembered nothing on the property was hers to lend.

This struck Albie at the same time, for he looked up to tell her almost alertly: 'Don't think I didn't put up a battle, but Miss Dianne's been 'ere with 'er boyfriend and got 'er ten bob's worth. If she wasn't a female, I coulda kicked 'er 'alf way across the yard. She put a lot of your aunt's stuff in the back o' the station wagon and I expect she'll be back for the rest.'

'What stuff?' Dean demanded, grimacing violently.

'Jest about everythin',' Albie returned fearlessly. 'I couldn't do nothin' but get flustered, and Camfield threatened to knock me block orf.'

'Small wonder!' Dean said scornfully, and heaved up an impatient sigh. 'I realise how loyal you are to Miss Lori, but you want to keep a lot of your opinions to yourself. It just so happens Miss Dianne inherited the property, and she has a perfect right to take what she likes!'

'Not the candlesticks, she ain't,' said Albie, paying close attention. 'They belong to Miss Lori and I said so!'

'Surely she didn't take those?' Lori asked him faintly.

'She sure did!' Albie snorted. 'Put 'em down ever so nice on the front seat. Soon as she left I grabbed the phone smartly to speak to Mr Elliot. Greedy little bitch—I remember what she was like as a kid; always jealous of Miss Lori and makin' trouble. I told 'er to wake up to herself. Don't think 'er dad wasn't goin' to change his will. I expect he woulda done that any day from now. You shoulda 'eard Camfield tryin' to square orf all the while. I don't know where he got the idea Miss Dianne would settle for 'im. Shouldn't be surprised with a temper like that she doesn't finish up an old maid!'

'Miss Lori said you can have the day off. Please go away!' Dean said stuffily, for his mood was contemptuous and he had never forgotten his last exchange with Albie. 'One thing more you might tell us. What has Elliot got to do with it?'

'Everythin',' Albie hissed succinctly. 'He's me boss now, you see, and he knows how to look out for a little slip of a girl. Besides which, it's only a matter of time before the farm passes into 'is 'ands. Does that answer your question, young feller?'

'You impertinent old devil!' snapped Dean, manoeuvring Lori out of the way.

'Be still, Albie!' cried Lori, grasping him firmly by the arm.

'I'll kill 'im!' Albie said modestly.

'Gently, gently,' she cautioned, feeling ready to collapse.

'Orright, jest whatever you say. I know you won't

bother about me not givin' notice. Mr Elliot offered me a job right away. Me and the dogs, and there are none better, look high an' low. They're working dogs, Miss Lori. I know you love them, but they're not suitable as pets.'

'No,' she said tiredly, convinced nothing more could hurt her. 'I'm glad you found yourself a job, Albie. Mr Elliot might work you a whole lot harder than I did!'

'I thought so meself!' Albie murmured with dignity. 'It's not the first time I've told yah, but I'm gonna tell you again. You're a grand girl, a real fighter. I don't like nuthin' about this will and I reckon yah can contest it. I'll even stand up in court for yah!'

'If you're sober, that is!' Dean said waspishly.

'A man is entitled to a drink as a consolation. Even Mr Elliot said that, but after today I'm gonna show me control!'

Dean muttered a disgusted 'pah!' and Lori pulled her bruised body up into the shade of the veranda. 'Are you coming back to the farm tonight, Albie?' she asked.

'Yes, ma'am. You should be in bed right now instead o' comin' over here, upsettin' yahself!'

'The fact is, I'm staying for a little while,' Lori explained. 'At least until I can get my things together and figure out what to do.'

'Don't worry about money,' Albie exclaimed grandly. 'I used to have a sister it went to, but you're welcome to it now. Not that I'm feelin' sorry for yah, I ain't. A spunky girl like you don't rate pity. I'm jest helpin' yah out from sheer admiration, that's the way it is. Never had a daughter. Matter of fact, I never got married, but you're right there up on a pedestal far as I'm concerned.'

'Oh, for God's sake!' Dean said shortly, and joined Lori on the veranda. 'Miss Lori has friends to help her out.'

'Here's a good one comin' now,' Albie breathed with some satisfaction. 'Reckon I can take myself orf now. See yah later, Miss Lori. Remember what I told yah. I'll never see yah stuck!'

Despite herself Lori had to smile. 'Thanks, Albie. I always said your heart's in the right place!'

'Me mum made sure o' that!' he said, and took his lanky frame off while Dean screwed his eyes up defensively and stared out at the fast approaching vehicle. It wasn't the station wagon this time, but the big powerful Mercedes 450.

'What the devil does he want?' Dean asked with disapproval.

'Haven't you been listening?' Lori said very quietly. 'Dianne has obviously signed some agreement. As Albie says, it's only a matter of time before Brant owns the place. He always vowed he'd get it—but even Brant didn't want it this way.'

'He doesn't own it yet!' Dean pointed out bitterly. 'Get rid of him.'

'No hope,' said Lori, and settled back in the old planter's chair. 'It's Brant's nature to get his own way in everything. I haven't the strength to fight him. Besides, I owe him my life.'

Dean turned back and stared at her, his pale face sombre and his blue eyes blazing. 'Surely you're not thinking of repaying him in some way? You're a very beautiful girl, and I know all about Elliot.'

'You exaggerate, Dean,' she said tiredly. 'Brant is a very fastidious man. Women might fling themselves at him, but I happen to know he's very selective.'

'And how would you know that?' Dean persisted in a cold, taut voice.

'Why are you so jealous of Brant?' she asked, and looked up at him with compassion.

'I just have this funny feeling about you and Elliot,' Dean said with a nervy restlessness. 'I don't like the way he looks at you, the hard vitality. There's a ruthlessness in him about getting his own way. Whatever the reason, neither of you are fooling me. If he doesn't want to marry you he wants you in some way. Him and his money. I still don't know how he got it all.'

'There's no success without a lot of hard work,' Lori offered gravely. 'How does anyone stop a dynamo? They're a special breed of men. Please don't start anything, Dean. You seem to be in a funny mood, and Brant's not Albie.'

'I don't like either of them,' Dean said soberly.

'Then try to be civil for my sake. Albie's right—I should be in bed. Trying to save me Brant nearly crushed me to death. There doesn't seem to be any part of my body that's not bruised, though I'm ashamed of complaining. He rode into stark horror to rescue me. I still have hideous nightmares about it.'

'And that's his attraction, is it?' Dean looked quickly back at her. 'He's the he-man type, isn't he? Twenty-four-carat gold, like that damned car.'

Lori was silent. Brant was pulling into the yard, parking incongruously alongside Dean's little red runabout. The recent heavy rain and the nightly thunderstorms had brought up dense green grass and transformed the trees laden with fresh new leaves, that normally Lori would have gloated over, but now she sat quietly waiting for Brant to come up to the veranda and join them.

She couldn't stop looking at him, even though he directed his 'good morning' at Dean. There was force and quality stamped all over him, the strength and character Dean was unwilling to concede. When he finally looked at her and she met the glinting blue-green gaze a faint colour swept under her skin. 'I'm sorry I didn't let you know I was leaving,' she offered a shade desperately.

'No, you're not,' he returned quite pleasantly. 'You make no sense at all, Lori, but now I'm here, you can tell me all about it.'

'Surely she doesn't have to explain herself to anyone?' Dean said baldly, and Brant redirected his brilliant, direct stare.

'I thought you mightn't have heard the news. Lori is going to marry me.'

Whatever answer he expected this completely floored Dean. 'I never knew,' he said thinly, and pushed back against the railing.

'Naturally it's no time to talk about it,' Brant answered quietly, 'but you might as well know.'

A quick anger was mounting in Dean. 'I won't believe it until I hear it from Lori. She seems remarkably quiet.'

Unthinkingly Lori passed her hand across her aching temples. 'Brant!' she said faintly. It was an appeal for help, but for once he wasn't listening.

'You don't seem very pleased about it, Dean?'

'I'm afraid I'm shocked,' said Dean, submerged in a jealous rage. 'I suppose this is an example of some of your storm tactics?'

'On the contrary,' Brant returned drily, 'it was decided when Lori told me she loved me.'

For a moment it seemed as if Dean would explode. His blue eyes sought Lori's face, receiving without words the extraordinary truth of the other man's statement, then he produced a short, bitter burst of laughter. 'When's the wedding supposed to be?'

'That's our affair,' was all Brant said.

'Do you really think you're going to take her away from me just like that?' Dean asked with a faint trace of hysteria.

'Don't lose your head,' Brant said to him. 'You've had years to talk of weddings. What's the use of squawking now when she's fallen in love with someone else?'

Dean started to laugh immoderately, hunching up his thin shoulders. 'You're lying. Lori's just sitting there saying nothing at all. You won't even let her make up her mind. Let her tell me freely she loves you and I'll go away for ever.'

'I'm sure she won't tell you she doesn't!' Brant looked briefly at Lori and away again.

Lori fought the wildest impulse to fly at him, to cry her denial, but he was overriding her with the power of his mind. Her whole body was aching and her brain was blurred with exhaustion and grief. 'You're a cruel devil, Brant!' she found the strength to whisper.

'Do you *love* him?' Dean prompted with violence.

'Yes!' she said wildly, and gave a gasp as her breath hurt her. 'Yes, oh *yes*!' She couldn't talk any more and she couldn't bear to be torn between both of them. Deeply upset, she pulled herself to her feet and rushed inside to collapse on to a sofa. The trembling shock of Brant's announcement was vibrating right through her nervous system. It was so easy for him to defeat her. Obviously he had wanted to spare her Dean's obsessive interest, but she wasn't going to be part of any of his grandiose gestures.

She didn't see Dean fling himself off the veranda with a backward glare of hate, but she heard the penetrating start of his car and the sound of it driven off in an uncontrollable rage. Then everything became quiet again. She was so agitated the heavy sofa seemed to be shaking, and when Brant walked into the room she gave a groan and buried her glowing head, looking so trapped and helpless she reminded him of a wild bird.

'Poor little Lori!' he said almost tonelessly. 'I had to do that. If you ask me Stanton's a little unbalanced. It wouldn't be right to sacrifice you.'

'I'm not exactly happy about it,' she whispered. 'It's an outrage!'

'For God's sake!' He sat down beside her and she pulled her feet under her, dangerously overwrought.

'I can't stand much more of this, Brant.'

'Neither can I!' He made no move to touch her. 'I'm not going to pressure you now, but make no mistake, I want you!'

'No,' she said, and arched away from him. 'Can you really see me as your wife?'

A brittle little smile touched his mouth. 'I know you're not old enough and I know you don't care enough, but the fact remains I'm prepared to take you just the way you are. I've been waiting to tell you since the first time I found you on my property.'

'But that's the first time we met!'

'So?' He looked at her with a kind of hard remoteness. 'Congratulations. You were—what, all of sixteen? Just old enough to make a fool of a man.'

'I don't believe it,' she said as though she was storing it up for working out later.

'I don't blame you. Don't think I've enjoyed having a slip of a girl getting under my skin. I hope you remember I've done nothing to frighten you, though I've had a bad time of it. Innocence alone made you completely inaccessible.'

Her eyes seemed drawn to him in complete fascination as if she heard but didn't understand a word he said.

'It's all right, little one!' he said with self-mockery. 'At the moment I'm only here to look after you. You look so fragile you'd probably break anyway.'

He went to stand up abruptly and Lori surprised herself by grasping at his hand. 'Don't go away,' she begged.

'I've no such intention!' he answered rather harshly. 'What on earth are you thinking about, being out of bed? You look dangerously frail.'

'I'm all right,' she said faintly. 'Bruised maybe, but that was a small price to pay. I've never thanked you for saving my life.'

'How do you imagine you might thank me?' he said swiftly.

'It's so difficult to speak to you sometimes,' she said plaintively. 'At least I try.'

He made a funny little gesture, almost of irritation and her eyes filled with tears. 'Why are you doing this for me, Brant? You're not sorry for me, are you?' To her horror the tears she had withheld were spilling on her cheek.

'*Don't cry*,' he said, unexpectedly violent.

'All right, then!' Frantically she brushed the tears away. 'I guess I do try your patience.'

Brant made some brief muffled exclamation and lowered himself beside her, his eyes intent on her face and the outline of her narrow body. 'Show me where I hurt you.'

The colour raced up under her pale golden skin,

and her eyes looked wary and huge. 'I'll never satisfy you, you know that.'

'Why, because you're afraid?'

She stared back at him and excitement was rising like waves through her body. 'Yes, I am,' she said simply. 'I might as well tell you. You've no idea how ... extraordinary you are. How forceful, as if you can have anything you want on demand.'

This remark apparently annoyed him, for his beautiful mouth hardened. 'I don't know whether I oughtn't to slap you for that.' He shifted slightly and lifted her with exquisite deliberation into his arms. 'I may have crushed you unintentionally the other day in a crisis, but otherwise I've always been on my very best behaviour. At any rate, you've nothing to complain about, so you can stop trembling, like the foolish child you are. I'm not going to ravish you this time either.'

'No, of course not.' She closed her eyes and tipped her head back to rest against his arm. 'Don't think I'm going to hold you to that rash promise to marry me either!'

'Little fool!' he murmured above her head.

'Would you mind if I went right off to sleep in your arms?' she asked him.

'I don't suppose it would hurt you,' he said drily. 'I can see the beginning of a bruise near your breast.'

'I've a hundred more to my credit,' she said, and shuddered soundlessly as his fingers loosened the drawstring that tied the shaped bodice of her sundress. 'Please, Brant,' she said, and her fingers quivered over his.

'I think *yes*,' he said, holding her amber eyes. 'Maybe kissing those bruises won't make them any better, but it's one way of saying I'm sorry.'

Her hand faltered and she tried to lie peacefully while his cool fingers pushed the bodice of her dress down. 'Lori!' he exclaimed almost painfully. 'Did I do that?'

'Why should you look at me when my skin is all bruised?' she said, helpless with a desire so acute she felt she might faint.

'You're beautiful!' he muttered, and put his mouth to the texture of her skin, while her body of its own accord became unbearably alive. The tenderness he was showing her, the control of his hands and his mouth was so powerfully erotic, she held herself closer, sighing over and over like a girl in a dream. She wasn't really frightened at all, her emotions were so completely in charge of her, she was actually urging him to take possession of her yearning body.

Instead he lifted his head and she found the strength to look up into his face. 'Have you decided I won't suit you at all?' she asked.

'I've decided I can't settle for half measures!' He curved his hand under her chin and held her face up. 'I know you've been trying to marry me off to Jane, but neither of us have ever felt in the least way romantic about one another. Something will work out for Jane—something my brother hopes for, at any rate. Right now I want you safely out of the way. You need a complete change and a holiday, and Jane tells me she's come up with the solution. Don't think I'm going to leave you here at the farm. You're coming back with me now and tomorrow or the next day I'll fly you and Jane and Ruth down to Brisbane. They'll see to it you're looked after, and I'd like you to buy a proper trousseau.'

'Maybe in Brisbane I'll forget all about you!' she

said a little wildly, disconcerted by his startling change from lover to Big Brother.

'We'll see!' he murmured with offhanded arrogance. 'By the way Dianne decided to return the silver candelabra.'

'What did you do to her?' she asked tightly.

'Not what I did to you anyway.' He lowered his head abruptly and caught her trembling mouth. 'If there's anything you want here, let's get it. After that, I'm taking you back to the house. That fool Stanton is just crazy enough to make a complete nuisance of himself. Here, let me help you.'

'I don't need you to help me dress myself,' she said, struggling and agonisingly shy again.

'You will!' he promised, and his voice seemed to tauten into ruthlessness. 'I haven't inexhaustible control. Remember that, when I come for you again.'

CHAPTER EIGHT

When Lori came up from the beach, she found Jane on the breakfast patio, scanning the morning paper. She looked up to greet Lori warmly, her eyes showing her pleasure in Lori's beautifully rested and relaxed appearance.

'How was the water?' she asked.

'Marvellous!' Lori smiled down at her, her jewel-coloured eyes lustrous with life. 'I think I'll have two slices of melon this morning. Is Ruth up?'

'Not after last night!' Jane said a little ruefully, and folded the paper in half. 'Some of my friends take an awful long time to go!'

'I like them.' Lori sank into a chair for a minute.

'I'll tell you this, they like you,' Jane returned with a laugh. 'Especially Marco.'

'Poor Marco!' Lori echoed. 'His charm is immense, but I could never take him seriously.'

'Just as well!' Jane said drily. 'If I understand my cousin correctly, you're absolutely committed to him.'

'So far in six weeks I've only had four phone calls,' Lori said rather crisply, looking down at her sun-glossed legs.

'Then we must presume he's busy,' said Jane, smiling a little at Lori's tone. 'Quite obviously you miss him.'

'Could it be possible he's not missing me?' Lori asked with the same hurt irritation threading her voice. 'For a while I honestly believed he might, but four phone calls, mostly checking up on what I've been doing, simply isn't enough! Most men planning on marrying behave in a certain way, but Brant isn't most men. Quite frankly I'm beginning to wonder if this unofficial engagement isn't one of his devilish jokes!'

Jane glanced at Lori's downbent head, her expression registering a certain sardonic amusement. 'Shall I tell him you're ready to see him? It sounds very much like it to me!'

'Oh, no!' Lori jumped precipitately to her feet. 'Let him come in his own good time. I really had no idea I sounded so nervy!'

'Not nervy, dear,' Jane amended. 'Sun and surf and good company won't satisfy a girl in love for ever. You sound frankly yearning, and I don't blame you. Brant can take orders as well as give them. Try him. Ring him and tell him you want him.'

Lori stood like a small wild creature bent on escape. 'I'll think about it,' she said shakily, pushing her hair off her face. 'I can't believe Brant loves me!'

Jane was horrified. 'Not love you?' she said, suddenly throwing her paper down on the grass, simultaneously frightening away all the little birds feeding ecstatically on breadcrumbs. 'You should take another look in the glass. You're pretty darned beautiful, and what's more important you're intelligent and loving. You're precisely the right kind of woman for Brant. You'll even be able to stand up to him, though you'll never be able to throw your weight around, I'll be thinking. Have a little faith, dear. You have everything going for you and you know perfectly well Brant won't change his mind. I mean, I *know* him, and I've grasped quite firmly that you'll never be allowed to run away from him. You're doubtless acquainted with his nature. I think you're a little sad and frightened because you're so young. Twenty, after all, isn't a great age.'

'It's a confusing one,' Lori said, somewhat heartened. 'I've enjoyed being here with you immensely, Jane. You and Ruth are simply the nicest people in the world.'

'You've been good for us too!' Jane insisted. 'What about a little shopping this morning?'

'Fine. I'll just have a quick shower and get the salt out of my hair.'

Jane's grey eyes narrowed over Lori's poised figure, slender and graceful in a brief two-piece swimsuit loosely covered by a sun-yellow wrap. The haunting delicacy of feature was still there, but not the extreme fragility, and Jane was proud of it. It had been necessary to get Lori away from the heartbreaking atmosphere of the farm. 'By the way, dear,' she said a little tentatively, 'Dean Stanton got a very good write-up for the Rachmaninoff on Saturday night.'

'I'm glad,' said Lori with a certain reserve.

'He's made no attempt to contact you, now he's in town?'

'As a matter of fact, he has. I was going to tell you about it. He wants me to meet him Wednesday night. He's giving a recital at the Conservatorium and he'd like me to be there.'

'Are you sure that's wise?' asked Jane, turning round in her chair and giving Lori her full attention. 'I have to admit something in his manner always made me a little uneasy. I know he's good-looking and very gifted and I know you've been friends for years, but he seemed very bitter about you and Brant. Brant gave me just a few of the details and he's holding me responsible for you.'

'I can't believe he would ever do anything to hurt or

embarrass me!' said Lori with the strength of all her old loyalty for Dean.

'I hope not!' Jane murmured. 'Surely he can come here. I'm reluctant to let you go to him.'

'It's only to the concert and a cup of coffee after-wards. Truly, Jane, I can handle Dean. He's a long familiar figure in my life and I wouldn't like to hurt him by totally rejecting him. It sounds very much as if he's on his feet again, and there's always his mother. Though Dean likes to deny it occasionally she's very important to him.'

'I think Mother and I will come along for protection,' Jane said so firmly that Lori burst out laughing.

'That will never do! Poor old Dean will be caught off balance. You don't think I'd go if I thought there was going to be any unpleasantness, Jane? He sounded his old self on the phone. He even asked after all of you, including Brant.'

Jane's blonde hair had come loose and she re-tied it with the silk scarf. 'It's easy to play games, and I don't think I quite trust him.'

'Jane, it will be all right!' Lori said softly. 'I'd better have breakfast if we're going to go shopping. Do you suppose we could go in to Surfers' Paradise? There's a super boutique I noticed the other day.'

'Why not?' Jane said more blithely. 'I just might be persuaded to buy something myself. If we wait an-other hour, Mother might feel fit enough to join us. You know how she hates to be left out, and she does have a gorgeous figure for a woman her age!'

'It's settled, then!' Lori flashed a smiling look over her shoulder. 'And, Jane,' she added gently, 'I'll be very careful with Dean!'

Lori took her place in the crowded auditorium and read up her programme. Everything from Bach to Bartok. She looked up again and let her eyes range over the audience. A preponderance of young people, a lot of them students, a fair sprinkling of the musical intelligentsia and the formidable domed head, entirely bald, of Dr Lloyd-Jones, the well-known composer and public enemy of all but the most genuinely gifted. If she had to play in front of *him*, Lori concluded, her nerves would be strained to breaking point, so coldly intent did he seem. At least he had found Dean's Saturday night performance technically flawless and artistically sound, though he accused the orchestra of occasional 'woodenness'. After all, it was his job to give an opinion.

Lori searched in vain for a glimpse of Mrs Stanton's rigidly handsome figure, then concluded that she must be somewhere behind the scenes. Dean's nerves were always ripped to shreds the agonisingly long moments before his fingers actually touched the keys, and Mrs Stanton was always on hand, surprisingly competent, a swift softening change coming over her glacial features, so that Lori, for one, scarcely recognised her on these occasions. The memory of some of these early occasions flashed through her mind, then clapping broke out all over the auditorium as Dean walked out on to the stage. His blue eyes glittered in his pale face and they ranged over the rows of seats until he found what he was looking for.

Lori, in her seat, drew a sharp breath, then Dean turned away to the piano, seated himself grandly, and the mask of professionalism slipped over his nerve-ridden face. There was no aura of crisis about Dean now. He began as splendidly as he finished the programme and Lori found herself clapping as enthusiastically as the young students on either side of her. Now that the concert was over, there was a smile on Dean's face and he looked very young and handsome, the light glinting on his blond hair, a flush under his smooth skin.

'He's good-looking, isn't he?' the young girl beside Lori turned to her to demand.

'Brilliant, too!'

'Umm!' she said, they both laughed. 'It's great when you can manage it!'

Lori could only agree. She smoothed the skirt of the blissfully pretty dress she was wearing and stood up to make her way backstage. Tonight seemed an essay into the past, but she felt she owed it to Dean. Her future belonged with Brant—that was if he ever came for her. She was terribly, hopelessly, madly in love with him, but she was not at all sure his feelings matched her own. Probably he was bored to distraction and had decided he wanted an heir. The very thought made the colour flare under her skin and she tried to pull herself together. It was absurd to be wanting Brant so badly when she was going to make pleasant conversation with Dean. That was the worst of loving a sophisticated older man. One never knew where one was, and apparently Brant was insensitive to her needs, otherwise why was he staying away so long?

As soon as Dean saw her he broke away from the congratulatory group around him and came towards her to grasp her two hands.

'Lori!' he said with his old endearing smile. 'You look absolutely fabulous!' His blue eyes went all over the green and gold garden print of the silk chiffon dress she and Jane had so carefully chosen. It was expensive and exquisitely right for Lori, accentuating her golden tan and her own lovely colouring.

'How are you, Dean?' she asked, cheered by his warmly affectionate greeting. 'Your performance was splendid. I think all of us are in entire agreement.'

'As a matter of fact Lloyd-Jones gave me a tiny nod of approval,' Dean replied, his high spirits infectious. 'Of course it might have had something to do with the fact that you were in the audience. I knew you wouldn't let me down.' The over-bright blue eyes rested on Lori intently.

'Where's your mother?' Lori asked briskly, wondering if she was mistaken about Dean's lighthearted manner.

'Back at the hotel. We're hoping you'll come back for a drink? Perhaps a little supper. I've had nothing all day!'

'Then you must be starving!'

'Oh, I *am*!' he said, and laughed shortly. 'Do say you'll come.'

'For half an hour,' she agreed. 'I have to drive back to the coast.'

'And how are they all?' Dean asked, and for an instant the pleasantness slipped.

'Fine. They've been very kind to me.'

'I'm not surprised. Some people are easy to be kind to. I'll just say goodnight here and we'll go.' He hurried away to make his farewells short.

They took Jane's car, which she had lent to Lori for the evening, and which was parked nearby, and in no time at all they were back at the hotel, taking the lift to the top floor.

'Your mother knows I'm coming, doesn't she?' Lori asked almost casually. For the first time in her life she felt completely indifferent about meeting Dean's mother.

For answer Dean smiled at her understandingly and inserted the key in the lock. 'You two always did make things unnecessarily complicated.'

'It seems to me that's not quite true, but never mind!'

'After you!' Dean stood back and gestured her into the room.

She couldn't refuse to go in, but something began to disturb her. 'It usually takes more than a headache to keep your mother away from your concerts,' she commented.

'That's right!' Dean said patiently, and closed the door behind them.

The room was quite empty and she walked to the adjoining sitting room, the bedroom door beyond, slightly ajar.

'Where is she?' she asked.

'She went home late this afternoon. Flew out in a towering rage.'

'You mean you were lying?'

'That's right! You wouldn't have come up with me otherwise.'

Lori's beautiful amber eyes began to blaze. 'And I was fool enough to believe you!'

Unexpectedly Dean laughed. He came up to her and took her by the shoulders. 'I always knew how you could look with a little care and money. Elliot's bought you, hasn't he?'

Her temper caught fire suddenly. 'I love him with all my heart!'

'Are you sure you know what love's all about?' Dean asked slowly, a sudden violence in the grip in her shoulders.

'Let go, Dean,' she said flatly. 'You're making a fool of yourself!'

'You're doing that!' he retorted, his blue eyes holding hers. 'I love you, Lori, and I can make you happy. Feelings can't change as easily as that. You've always cared for me, you know you have!'

'As a good friend!' she stressed with a decided show of spirit. 'I've always believed in you, your ability, but I don't love you. I can't love you. Brant is the only man in the world I want.'

'Then where is he now?' Dean almost yelled at her. 'If he wants you as much as you seem to think, why isn't he here with you? He's no fool. He wants a beautiful young wife, just another piece for the showcase. You're really very dense, and he's a hard, shrewd man. And why *you*?' he raged at her. 'Di made quite a play for him and she's a sophisticated beauty. No, he wanted a sweet silly little kid like you.'

Lori shook her gleaming head and her look of spirit seemed to fade. 'For whatever reason Brant offered marriage I'm not going to accept it unless I'm sure he loves me for myself.'

'Oh, his reason's clear enough,' Dean sneered, 'but it's not love. Lust, maybe. He can live without you. *I* can't!'

His kissed her then, his lips full of heat and violence, his moody young face white with the intensity of his feelings. 'I'll make you forget!' he murmured angrily against her mouth. 'Oh, Lori, Lori darling!'

His embrace was becoming suffocating and Lori's head began to swim. He was very strong and he was pushing her with the violence of his desire towards the bed, absorbed in his need for conquest. With rising panic she began to wonder how she could get away from him. This was the stuff nightmares were made of, and his intentions were plain. She tried to say his name, anything to calm him, but the pressure of his mouth strangled the breath in her throat. Fool that she was, when even Jane had been aware of the danger. Dean had her down on the bed with his lean body poised over her, his blue eyes glittering.

'Swear you'll stay with me!'

'You're mad!' She stared up at him.

'Maybe I am, just a little!' His strong pianist's hands slipped around her throat. 'Lori!' he said very softly.

'Let me go!'

Very gently he applied a little pressure to her windpipe.

'Dean, *stop*!' she begged.

It came out in a little husky cry and his fingers eased immediately. 'Stay here with me tonight. Why should Elliot have you?'

It was so quiet in the room Lori could hear her heart beating wildly. 'I want to go, Dean. Let me up!'

'Why?' he demanded with ferocity. 'Why, Lori? You've let Elliot make love to you.'

'He doesn't use force! He doesn't *have* to!'

She knew the minute the words left her mouth she had made a dreadful mistake. Dean gave her a strange look and glanced involuntarily at his hands. 'I could kill you,' he said in a half strangled voice. 'I've got nothing to lose. The world is full of concert pianists, top internationals. I mean if I had you I could work hard. You matter to me more than anything, I realise that now.' He shook his head sharply as if to clear it. His lips were trembling and he said to her defiantly, 'I'm sorry it's got to be like this ...'

The phone shrilled suddenly in the quiet room and Dean straightened up and looked around.

'Hadn't you better answer it?' Lori swung up and

tried to get to her feet, but Dean held her back with his hand.

'Stay where you are.'

'Quite obviously someone knows you're here!'

'Be quiet! I want to try to think.'

'The sooner you do that, the better!' she said, pulling herself upright. 'We aren't alone on a desert island. There are people all round us. I can't believe even now you would mean to hurt me.'

'What I want is your promise to stay with me, and I don't care very much how I get it!'

She looked at his face and his blond hair and his unblinking blue eyes. There was a curious alertness about the set of his body, though his smile was almost calm. 'There, it's stopped!'

'It won't be easy!' she said levelly. 'Rape is an act of violence.'

'I suppose so.' He seemed to hesitate, then he looked down at her and the dark rush of excitement showed in his face. The phone rang again, then there was a knock on the door—no discreet tap but a hard rap, demanding entry.

'It looks rather as if someone wants to come in!' Lori said rapidly, waiting her moment, willing herself out of the tremors that gripped her.

Dean's face was set in angry, indecisive lines. 'Who's there?' he called, and turned his head towards the door.

In an instant Lori was on her feet, flying across the plush carpet, reaching for the key a little wildly, finding it, turning it with Dean's hard hand on her shoulder, his pallor alarming. The door was shoved hard from the other side, then Brant was looking at them, completely terrifying in his height and power, his brilliant gaze slanting over their stricken faces.

'What the hell goes on?' he demanded harshly, and Dean slumped back and started to laugh.

'The troops have arrived!'

'Somebody better tell me,' said Brant grimly, easing his back against the closed door.

'Nothing,' said Lori, and his eyes narrowed over her.

'God knows you're young, but I didn't think you were a fool. Haven't I warned you about Stanton?'

'Nothing's happened to her!' said Dean, the hysterical laughter abruptly switched off.

'You wanted a little more time?' Brant asked in the kind of voice that made Lori look at him aghast.

'Really, Brant, everything is all right.'

'I'll decide that!' He looked directly at her and his eyes had darkened to a brilliant, cold emerald.

'Please let's just *go*!' she begged, brushing her hair back.

'Could it be you want to?'

She moved across to him, her small face pleading, too frightened to touch his arm. 'Please, Brant, don't let's have any trouble. I'm sorry!'

His flashing look of scorn silenced her. 'Go downstairs and wait in the lobby.'

She took a deep steadying breath, her topaz eyes burning with tears of fright. 'I don't want you to hurt Dean. He knows nothing about ...'

'Will you *go*!' Brant repeated, towering above her. 'I won't hit him hard!'

Dean muttered something almost unintelligible about being a pianist, slumped in the background, looking so white and tormented Lori was surer than ever he needed protection. Brant looked incredibly menacing, his fury controlled but white-hot. Dean would never know what had hit him. In fact he was already folding, and she could feel his humiliating pain. It wasn't in her to punish him, though she had found his behaviour contemptible.

'If you want to hit anyone, hit me!' she said shakily.

'I might find it agreeable to turn you over my knee.' Brant's eyes flicked over her, appraising her, then he took her by the shoulders and put her out the door.

She went. There was nothing else she could do. No sound had come from the room by the time the lift arrived and she closed her eyes all the way down to the ground floor. Considering the way Dean had acted, some kind of reprisal was due, but they were so hopelessly mismatched. Brant was a big man and Dean was surprisingly lightweight. Lori stood uncertainly in the lobby for a moment, then went to sit down. There didn't seem to be a soul around and she was glad of it. Her own involvement had been quite innocent, yet Brant had made her feel guilty of a capital crime.

A few minutes later the other lift descended and she quelled a sudden tremor in her hands. Brant came through the opening doors and walked towards her, taking her nerveless hands and pulling her to her feet.

'Let's go!'

He compelled her through the entrance and down into the car park. 'Where's the car?' He swung on her, his dark face relentless.

'Over there.' She pointed away to Jane's Triumph, her mind in a tumult. 'What did you do to Dean?'

'He took it like a little man!' he murmured unpleasantly.

'You didn't hurt him?'

He ignored her, taking her small evening purse and hunting up the car keys. 'I didn't realise . . .' she began halfheartedly.

'Well, well!' was all he said as he unlocked the passenger side and almost thrust her in.

There was no conversation whatever as he backed out and pulled the car into the line of traffic. 'Where the devil is the seat release?' he asked irritably. 'I'm not looking for an accident.' In an instant he had found it, shoving the seat back to accommodate his long legs, muttering something about little women driving cars. The overhead street lighting slanted across his profile and it looked extremely aggressive, more: *disquieting*. There was no softness about cleft chins.

'If you don't want to speak to me, I'll get out!' Lori breathed jerkily.

'Try it.'

'It would help a great deal if you'd let me explain.'

'Go right ahead!' said Brant in a brutally cool tone.

'I'm almost afraid to!'

'Not you, Lori,' he said jeeringly, 'you're quite a spunky little thing. I even prefer you that way.'

'I doubt it!' she said emotionally. 'You like a yes-woman in everything.'

'Which, of course, is what you were saying to Stanton?'

She spun her bright head, her amber eyes shimmering. Don't be ridiculous!'

'Then what the devil *were* you doing?'

'Dean acted a little foolishly, that's all.'

'*Dean* did?' he said with the utmost sarcasm. 'I could pertinently say you acted like a complete little fool. Jane tried to guide you, having a cooler and wiser head, but you wouldn't listen. Compassionate little Lori had to race off to hold Stanton's hand. And then if everything worked out all right, to sleep with him!'

Bright tears sprang into her eyes and caught in her lashes. 'I thought you'd say that!'

'I couldn't resist it, but no matter. I'd say I got there just in time. A very interesting type, Stanton. We'd better blame it onto his mother. We won't be seeing either of them for a very long time.'

'At least he wanted to marry me,' Lori said wryly.

'You took that on good faith, did you?'

'Yes,' she said, 'you sarcastic brute! He did really.'

'It seems hardly fair you're going to marry me.'

'Let's talk about something else, shall we?' she said, and her skin flushed apricot.

'Though I must admit you've given me some cause for doubt.'

'I'm sure you're free to change your mind,' she said furiously.

'But *you're* not!' He reached out a hand and gripped her arm. 'You're my property, make no mistake.'

'I'm not property, I'm a woman!' she snapped.

'Just barely. The minute I turn my back you seem to come to some harm. It's a damned good thing Jane was worried and rang me to say so. It was a high-powered ride to get up to town, and I haven't even levelled off yet. So don't expect me to say sweet things to you. I'm only keeping my hands off you by sheer effort of will. Perhaps after this, you'll think twice about placing yourself in a hazardous position. Nothing would have saved Stanton had he touched you. He's so weak, so damned weak—and a very unsatisfactory man to hit.'

'Oh, for God's sake!' Lori gave a convulsive little shudder. 'Poor Dean!'

A flash of anger crossed Brant's face. 'You've got an odd slant if anyone has. Aren't you at all particular who rapes you?'

'He didn't touch me!' she said, her throat curiously dry.

'Because, my poor little innocent, I got there in time. Forgive me if I see these things differently.'

She averted her head and there were tears on her cheeks. 'I said I was sorry. I just like to think of people as being good. Dean was my friend. I thought I could trust him.'

'You haven't had enough dealings with men to know them. For safety's sake, from now on I'm going to keep you close beside me. If you hadn't been at the hotel I don't know what I'd have done. Jane couldn't tell me much except it was a concert at the Conservatorium. I just missed it, but at least someone gave me the address of his hotel, so I took the chance.'

He looked and sounded a hard, dangerous man, and his anger was pressing on her like an actual weight. 'It just so happens I can defend myself!' she said with some passion. 'I've got two arms and two legs and I can yell my head off!'

'Oh, really?' He pulled the car off the highway and nosed the bonnet into the tree-lined shadows. 'Let's see!' He switched off the engine and turned on her, his eyes gleaming in the white radiance of moonlight.

'Don't be silly!' Lori pushed right back against the door.

'You silly little rabbit!'

'I know you're always trying to help me, but I think I'll hitch a ride.'

'Exactly my point. You do one crazy thing after another.'

'Well, I try,' she supplied rather helplessly. 'I think I would always disappoint you, Brant. In fact I don't think you really like me!'

'Oh, I do,' he assured her, very cool and detached. 'You're all I think about.'

She gave a strangled little cry and felt for the door handle. 'Why don't you pick a fight with someone who has a chance?'

'It's much too late in the day for that!' He flung a hand behind her and locked the door. 'I happen to love you, though I'm perfectly well aware you don't want to be loved.'

'Unless it's for myself!' she said fervently. 'I want to be loved for myself!'

'Forgive me if I'm puzzled. I don't think I mentioned anyone else?'

'It's nothing to laugh about,' she said with considerable vehemence.

'I'm not laughing exactly,' said Brant, and reached for her, stroking the satiny curve of her cheek with his forefinger.

'No. Leave me alone. Go away!'

'When I want your opinion I'll ask for it. Come here to me and be still. There's no way to talk sense to a woman until she's absolutely quiet!' He lifted her right into his arms and the serene radiance of the moon touched her face, infintely desirable, the tender mouth melancholy, her eyes looking away from him.

'I'm not really clever enough for you!' she persisted.

'We must have a good long talk about it.'

'There's a considerable difference in our ages.'

'Is that what's making you so nervous?' He was shaping her nape, tilting her head back.

'Did Stanton kiss you?'

'I don't remember.'

There was a tiny painful jerk on her hair and her

almond eyes flew to him. 'I assure you I protested all the time. I think men are horrible in general!'

'Oh, there are a few good ones,' he murmured. 'Why don't you admit it?'

'If there are, they're old gentlemen with long beards!'

His low laugh touched her ears, some special magic in it that made her say humbly: 'It was all my fault with Dean. I didn't know. I thought his mother would be with him. I didn't know she'd gone home.'

'Yes, of course. I believe you, little one. You've just got to give me time to simmer down. Stanton mightn't have frightened you badly, but he sure frightened me. I doubt very much if you know what I'm talking about.'

Lori curled her fingers tightly around his, the vibrant warmth of him suddenly made her relax deeply. 'I've missed you desperately!' she whispered.

'Really?' his tone was very dry, the brilliant eyes watchful, intent on her face. 'When was this exactly?'

'Every day.'

'Why didn't you just sing out?' he asked rather tersely.

'Because I can't for the life of me believe you love me. Do you, Brant?'

'How can you doubt it?' he asked quietly. 'I loved you long ago when you were just a courageous little girl with the great promise of beauty. I couldn't have told you then, it wasn't the time, but I can tell you now. You're everything I want in a woman, sweet and compassionate and tender. You've got character. You feel things, respond to them. You're as vital as a flame. You're a fighter too, which I consider important. Not that I've any intention of falling on hard times, but I know you'll be there with me no matter what happens.

And lastly, and I can't deny it, I love you because you're the most desirable woman I've ever known. I want to make you a part of me, my own. I want to discover every least little thing about you, your body and your mind. Does that answer your question?'

'Yes, it does rather!' she said, but there was a deep intensity in her voice. 'I adore *you*!'

Brant made a sudden little movement and cupped her face in his hands. 'My beautiful girl!'

'Love me,' she whispered, with no thought of checking him.

'I've done that a million times already in sleep.' He lowered his dark head abruptly and covered her mouth with his own, while she gave herself up to the fabulous feeling of rightness, of truly belonging. She loved him with a passion and tenderness that moved her so deeply, she began to murmur ardent little endearments into his mouth, the slender contours of her body fitting his hard frame with such absolute beauty and perfection she might have been made for him alone. The minutes slipped by, so inexpressibly beautiful she was shaking in his arms.

'Are you going to marry me?' he murmured against her throat.

'Of course! Don't let it be long.'

He lifted his dark head to look down at her. 'How could I when I want you so badly?'

'So do I!' she said childishly, and he laughed at the astonishing urgency of her tone.

'Good.' He kissed her once more with his hard, beautiful mouth, then put her back in her seat, valiantly resisting his own driving longings. 'It just isn't possible to make love to you in a car, and I'm damned if the first time isn't going to be just right. Which means the night I marry you. Can you wait?'

'Oh yes!' Lori said firmly, blinking away the quick emotional tears caused by his lovemaking. 'Patience has its own reward, surely?'

'It has indeed, my darling,' he said drily. 'I've waited long enough for you.' He lifted her hand to kiss it and when she turned to him her smile was piercingly sweet. All the love in the world shone out of her lovely amber eyes.

It was wonderful to come home. The most heartwarming feeling in the world. Brant was her future. There could be no other way.

Harlequin

COLLECTION
EDITIONS OF 1978

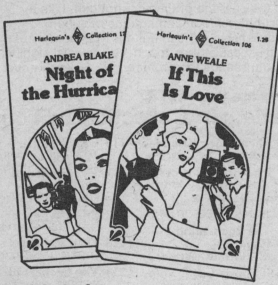

**50 great stories
of special beauty
and significance**

$1.25
each novel

In 1976 we introduced the first 100 Harlequin Collections—a selection of titles chosen from our best sellers of the past 20 years. This series, a trip down memory lane, proved how great romantic fiction can be timeless and appealing from generation to generation. The theme of love and romance is eternal, and, when placed in the hands of talented, creative, authors whose true gift lies in their ability to write from the heart, the stories reach a special level of brilliance that the passage of time cannot dim. Like a treasured heirloom, an antique of superb craftsmanship, a beautiful gift from someone loved—these stories too, have a special significance that transcends the ordinary. **$1.25 each novel**

Here are your 1978
Harlequin Collection Editions...

Original Harlequin Romance numbers in brackets

ORDER FORM

Harlequin Reader Service

In U.S.A.
MPO Box 707
Niagara Falls, N.Y. 14302

In Canada
649 Ontario St.,
Stratford, Ontario, N5A 6W2

Please send me the following Harlequin Collection novels. I am enclosing my check or money order for $1.25 for each novel ordered, plus 25¢ to cover postage and handling.

☐ 102	☐ 115	☐ 128	☐ 140
☐ 103	☐ 116	☐ 129	☐ 141
☐ 104	☐ 117	☐ 130	☐ 142
☐ 105	☐ 118	☐ 131	☐ 143
☐ 106	☐ 119	☐ 132	☐ 144
☐ 107	☐ 120	☐ 133	☐ 145
☐ 108	☐ 121	☐ 134	☐ 146
☐ 109	☐ 122	☐ 135	☐ 147
☐ 110	☐ 123	☐ 136	☐ 148
☐ 111	☐ 124	☐ 137	☐ 149
☐ 112	☐ 125	☐ 138	☐ 150
☐ 113	☐ 126	☐ 139	☐ 151
☐ 114	☐ 127		

Number of novels checked @
$1.25 each = $ _____

N.Y. and N.J. residents add
appropriate sales tax $ _____

Postage and handling $ ___.25

TOTAL $ _____

NAME _____
                    (Please Print)
ADDRESS _____

CITY _____

STATE/PROV. _____

ZIP/POSTAL CODE _____

ROM 2203

Offer expires December 31, 1978

And there's still *more* love in

Harlequin Presents...

Yes!

Four more spellbinding
romantic stories every month
by your favorite authors.
Elegant and sophisticated tales of
love and love's conflicts.

Let your imagination be swept away to
exotic places in search of adventure,
intrigue and romance. Get to
know the warm, true-to-life
characters. Share the special
kind of miracle that
love can be.

Don't miss out. Buy now and discover
the world of HARLEQUIN PRESENTS...

Do you have a favorite
Harlequin author?
Then here is an
opportunity you must
not miss!